DON'T TACO 'BOUT MURDER

MONA MARPLE

With special thanks to Jeff Elkins (The Dialogue Doctor) for your help on this book!

Thank you to my advance readers who help spot those pesky typos!

AUTHOR NOTE

As an English author, I write in English (not American English). You may notice that I use 's' where American English would use 'z', in words such as realising. Colours here have that 'u' in them.

Believe it or not, this book (published in January 2021) is one I started writing in July 2019.

In that first version, the characters found themselves running a Mexican restaurant in an English seaside town. This book is very different (and, I hope, better!).

The 2019 version had to be placed to one side while my own life had some ups and downs, and then the whole world fell apart with COVID19.

I hope you are healthy, safe and loved, and that reading is a comfort to you in these strange times. I know it is to me.

With blessings and thanks for giving my books a chance,

Mona x

1

Standing in the long queue to hand over our luggage, I had to pinch myself to make sure I wasn't dreaming.

"This is so cool," I murmured.

Uncle Cornelius chuckled at the side of me. "I'm glad you think so, lassie. I happen to agree. Can you believe that we'll be up above the clouds shortly? It's a modern-day miracle!"

"I can't even imagine it," I said as we moved a few steps forward along with the rest of the line.

The airport was a hustle bustle of action. We were in a large open space surrounded by hundreds of people who formed a dozen or more human snakes as they waited for their turn at the baggage drop.

I couldn't stop staring. My fellow jet setters were dressed in a rainbow of colours and styles. It was winter in England and I'd dressed appropriately, but it seemed as though a lot of people had dressed ready for the place they were travelling to, with little shorts and t-shirts, flip flops and hats.

"They must be freezing," I whispered.

Cornelius laughed. "The excitement will keep them warm! Not to mention the blankets."

"Blankets?"

"On the plane. They hand out blankets. It gets pretty cold up there," Cornelius explained.

I giggled at the thought of me flying through the sky wrapped up in a blanket.

Another person moved to the baggage drop and we stepped forward. We were nearly at the front of the queue. There was just a group of young men in fancy dress between us and the baggage drop desks.

"It's a real explosion of colour in here, isn't it?" I asked.

One of the men in front of us in the queue turned and peered at me. He had a curly blonde wig on and a very impressive fake bosom. I averted my gaze.

"Now isn't the time to talk about explosions, lassie. Also, don't pretend you asked a stranger to watch your luggage," Uncle Cornelius explained.

"Why would I do that?" I asked.

"Just don't. These security staff have no sense of humour."

"Okay," I assured him.

The fancy dress stag party had only one suitcase between them all, and were quickly on their way.

The woman at one of the baggage desks beckoned me over, and a young man at the desk next to her gestured for Cornelius.

"The purpose of your travel today, ma'am?" A young woman with the whisper of a moustache above her upper lip asked from beside her desk.

"I'm going on holiday!" I grinned at her.

"Mm-hmm," the woman looked between the me

standing in front of her and the me on a photo in my brand-new passport.

"I'm going to Mexico. I've never left England before! I'm very excited!" I leaned in and whispered. I knew it was immodest to boast but I had to talk about it. I hoped my mother would forgive me if she was watching over me.

"You're travelling alone today?" She asked with a sigh.

"Oh, no," I explained. I looked across at the next booth, where my 70-year-old uncle was answering his own set of questions. "That's my Uncle Cornelius, we're travelling together."

The woman leaned forward in her seat and frowned a little. "That's your uncle?"

I nodded. "Yep. That's Uncle Cornelius. There was a... erm... my mum was quite a bit younger."

Sitting forward and peering over her glasses at Uncle Cornelius, the lady said, "Ma'am, are you under any pressure to travel today against your wishes?"

"What? No!" I exclaimed, then lowered my voice. "This is absolutely going to be the greatest trip ever. I've been watching TV shows about it, and it's all sandy beaches and relaxation. I couldn't be more excited. Plus, apparently I'm going to learn some things about my mother over there."

"Your mother lives in Mexico" The security woman raised an eyebrow.

"No, no. She's English and she's actually dead, but my dad's alive. I've been living with Uncle Cornelius for a while. See, he's helping me see some different sides of the world. Don't get me wrong, my parents were amazing, but I'd never really had an adventure before Uncle C. That's what I call him, Uncle C. He says I'll learn some things about my mum in Mexico," I felt myself begin to sweat. Uncle Cornelius had finished at the other booth, but I couldn't catch his eye because his attention was on his mobile phone.

"Ma'am, I just need to know if you're visiting family in the country," the woman said.

"Oh! No! Just a holiday."

"Ma'am, I'm going to ask you to follow my colleague here. Your Uncle too," the woman said, and a large man with a neck wider than his head gave me a short nod.

I gulped. "Have I done something wrong?"

"Don't you worry, we'll get this cleared up," the man said. He cleared his throat as we approached Uncle Cornelius, who reluctantly moved his attention away from the latest model gadget in his hand. "Sir, follow me please."

"What's happening?" I whispered as we were lead along a corridor and then through a keypad secured door into another corridor.

"Don't worry, lassie," Cornelius stroked his beard as he spoke. "They probably heard that we're a couple of VIP travellers! We certainly look the part. My hand luggage alone makes it clear that we're a family of good taste and fine heritage. I bought this bag from a market stall in Gibraltar years ago. Rupert, the man's name was. I remember him to this day. He told me never to buy another hand luggage bag. If the bag broke, he insisted I return it to him and he would repair it free of charge. A lifetime guarantee, I guess. Isn't that something?"

"And have you? Ever taken it back?" I asked, relieved to have something to focus on other than the man leading us away from the main concourse in silence.

"Well, no, I've never been back to Gibraltar. But still, a fine offer. A fine offer."

"In here, please," the security guard held open a door and we entered. There was a small table with two seats on each side, and with a tilt of his head, the guard made it clear he wanted me and my uncle to sit together on one side.

He sat across from us and cracked his knuckles, then looked at each of us in turn.

"Travel destination?" He asked. There was no apology for the intrusion to our day, no small talk about the weather, and no offer of a cup of tea. He was so direct and to the point, I wondered if he really was English.

"Mexico," I said.

"Mexico City," Cornelius said.

"Purpose for travel?"

"We're going on holiday," I said.

"We'll conduct a little family research too. Emily here, her mum has some history in Mexico. It's her first time travelling abroad, you know. I'd hate for her to have any bad memories of the trip. You never forget your first time, do you? I'm sorry, I didn't catch your name?" Cornelius said.

"You don't need my name," the guard said with a grunt.

Uncle Cornelius laughed and said, "I certainly do. How am I supposed to address you if I don't have your name?" Turning to me he added, "What? Should we just call him nameless guard?"

"What about this trip do you think will leave her with bad memories?"

Uncle Cornelius gave a little chortle. "I mean this right here. Bringing us down this corridor and into this room, not even so much as giving us your name. It's the kind of thing that might make Emily consider flying from a different airport in future."

The guard stiffened a little at that suggestion.

"There's a rival airport just across the city, Emily," Cornelius continued. "We'll use them next time we fly."

I grinned, despite the unnerving situation. I was very

excited to hear the suggestion that there would be future travel! More airports in my future! What a thrill!

"There'll be no need for that," the guard said. He cracked a smile for the first time. It sat unnaturally on his pale face. "I'm sure when selecting your airport of preference, you want the airport that has your security as the priority."

"Well, of course," Cornelius agreed.

"If you could just run through it with me. Where you're travelling and why, and then I'm sure you can be on your way."

Uncle Cornelius cleared his throat. "We're heading to Mexico, my niece and I. It's a holiday, you could say. And we're going to Mexico because it's a place that was dear to Emily's mother's heart. She's passed now, God rest her soul."

"And you are?"

"I'm her uncle. That's why I said my niece and I."

"Big age difference between the two of you," the guard said with a frown.

"Not that big!" Cornelius objected. "It's the beard, it ages me. I'm only seventy, I'll have you know."

"And where are you going on this holiday?"

"We're flying to Mexico City," Cornelius said. "We have a few nights in the metropolis and then we move to a resort. It's all booked and paid for. Do you want to see the bookings?"

The guard gave a slight nod of his head and Uncle Cornelius grabbed his mobile phone and tap-tapped away, then offered the device to the guard, who leaned in and gave a sigh.

"You've been to Mexico before?"

"Well, no," Cornelius admitted.

"You haven't?" I whispered, eyes wide.

"I've seen a lot of programmes about it, and I love The Power and the Glory, of course. Graham Greene. Have you read it? Very interesting book it is. I highly recommend it. Maybe they'll have a copy in W H Smith."

The guard tried to mask a smirk and shook his head. "Okay, I'm satisfied that you two are telling me the truth. You can go on your way. You know where you're heading?"

"Yes, yes, of course," Cornelius said as he rose to his feet.

I did the same and held my hand out to the guard, who gave it a quick shake as he opened the door for us. He led us back down the corridor and out onto the busy main concourse. Travellers milled around in a constant buzz of excitement. It was intoxicating.

"Well, thank you for your help," I said.

"Yes, thank you sir. Good day to you!" Cornelius exclaimed.

"That was weird," I said.

"I know! Only the English would thank a stranger for detaining them without reason. I've had worse, though. I was manhandled once and searched by quite a frisky young attendant. I swear she just liked the look of me. I was younger then, of course. What would I have been? Only fifty I reckon. I was quite the sight for sore eyes, lassie."

I grinned at the story. "I bet you were. What do we do now? We've still got two hours before the flight time."

"The world is our lobster now! Well, inside the airport is, anyway. We'll get through security and then we can look around the shops, get a bite to eat. Are you hungry? My belly's rumbling and it'll be hours before they feed us on the plane."

"They feed us on the plane?" My mouth gaped open.

Uncle C laughed. "They sure do. Although the portion's

aren't designed for a growing man like me. Let's have something now, shall we?"

"Sure!" I exclaimed.

We got through security without being manhandled, much to Cornelius' disappointment, and found a pub - a real, actual pub inside the airport! - and both ordered a full English breakfast.

"Filled a hole, eh, lassie?" Cornelius beamed as I dipped a corner of toast into my egg yolk. His plate was already empty, despite him ordering the larger Belly-Buster portion.

"It's delicious!" I enthused.

"You're a natural traveller, I can tell," he said with a wink.

"Really? Wow, thank you! It feels good to be making this trip like my mum did. I can't imagine her as an eighteen-year-old."

Uncle Cornelius smiled. "She was one in a million. She was so excited to go off and see the world. As soon as her friend mentioned Mexico, that was it, your mother was saving every penny she could beg, steal or borrow. She had this piggy bank - a real pig it was. Well, not a real pig. It didn't walk around oinking. But it was really shaped like a pig. You know what I mean. I was already working by then, of course, had my own money coming in. I slipped her a few pound coins here and there when I could."

"That's really sweet," I felt my eyes water as I imagined my mother wanting something so badly, and Uncle Cornelius secretly helping her achieve it. "What happened between you two? She never told me any of these stories."

"Don't you worry about that. All will be revealed."

"Will it be revealed on this trip?"

Uncle Cornelius chewed a last piece of black pudding and considered the question. "Yes, lassie, hopefully it will. It's time."

"You can't just tell me now?"

He shook his head, jowls wobbling. "Don't rush it. I will tell you everything, I promise. But there are some things you need to experience first, so as it all makes sense."

I wanted to push for more information but I knew I couldn't. I'd spent my whole life aware of a rift that stopped my mother speaking to Uncle Cornelius, but I had no idea what had caused it.

One thing was for sure - once I knew whatever Uncle C had to reveal, I would never be able to unknow it. People say that ignorance is bliss, and I was going to find out once and for all whether that was really the case.

UNCLE C'S WORLD WIDE WEB LOG

A short and sweet first entry on this web log because I am about to board a plane!

Yes, your intrepid travel web logger is off to faraway places in search of new faces.

I'm travelling with E, my niece. She is much younger than I am but somehow I am the Tech Guru between the two of us! In an act of respect for her reluctance to go viral, I am only referring to her as her initial.

Or maybe E isn't even her initial. Who knows?!

The world wide web is, after all, a maze of secrets and confusion.

But, fear not, dear reader, for I shall not lead you wrong.

E (or not E) and I are about to board a plane to Mexico City, where I expect we will find the sun loungers with the best available spots, and do nothing but relax.

Who am I kidding?

No doubt we'll find adventures we can't even begin to comprehend.

That's all for now, fans.

Asta la vista,
Uncle C

2

———————

I accepted Uncle Cornelius' offer of the window seat without even a moment's hesitation, which wasn't very polite, especially since Uncle C had paid for the whole trip. But any regret I'd felt about my lack of manners disappeared as soon as I looked out of the window onto the tarmac.

Airport workers in hi-vis vests milled around, speaking into radios or waving their arms. Lorries drove - actually drove! - on the ground by the airplane, transporting suitcases into the hold. I peered out, trying to spot my own case, but I couldn't.

"Ours are already on there, lassie," Cornelius guessed what I was doing.

"They are?"

He nodded. "We arrived in plenty of time, our bags will be tucked up safe for us. Those last few cases are for the stragglers. There's always a few people who arrive late and just make it by the skin of their teeth!"

"Wow. I can't imagine ever daring to arrive late," I said.

"And that's exactly right, because trust me a plane will go when it's ready, whether you're here or not."

"Seriously? You mean if we'd been late today the plane wouldn't have waited?"

Cornelius chuckled. "No way, lassie. A plane waits for nobody!"

"But we have tickets. You've paid a lot of money for them, I'm sure," I flushed a little at the mention of the money that Uncle C had spent on our trip.

"It doesn't matter. The plane will set off without any passengers who are late. Even very special passengers like you and I," he said with a wink.

"Wow. That's unbelievable. Have you been on many planes?" I asked.

"Dozens over the years. I thought it would stop being fun at some point but it never has. It's a miracle, a real life miracle! All of us people, all of this weight, plus our baggage, and the plane itself, and it really flies! It somehow stays up in the sky!"

I gave a nervous smile.

"Oh! Lassie! Are you okay? You've gone a little green. Has that brekkie upset your stomach?"

"No, no, I'm fine. I guess I just realised that we're actually going to be in the sky."

"Don't you worry. It's perfectly safe. Hardly any planes crash! Most of them don't have any issues at all."

"Most of them?" I asked.

"Yes! Virtually all of them are perfectly safe. And even the ones that aren't, well, they have inflatables and things. Do you remember hearing about the pilot in New York a few years ago? He realised the engines had failed or something and he landed the plane in the river!"

"In the river?" I asked as my stomach churned.

"Yes! In the river! Incredible, it was. So it's possible to survive a plane crash, you see."

"Goodness," I murmured to myself as I reached for the sick bag that had been handily provided along with the blanket and ear phones.

"In fact, let me try and find the clip of that plane. It's quite the sight, lassie!" Cornelius continued on. He pulled his phone out of his pocket and began tap-tapping away.

I watched, frozen in horror as I realised that Uncle C was about to show me a plane crash just before our plane took off.

A flight attendant saved the day by leaning in to us as she did her final checks. "Sir, turn your phone off please."

Uncle Cornelius flashed me an apologetic smile as I breathed a sigh of relief.

We both buckled up, and Uncle Cornelius had leaned back and began to snore within seconds.

I watched the safety demonstration, read the in flight magazine from front to back, watched out of the window as we left the ground and inclined our way up into the sky. I gasped as the cars on the motorways grew smaller and smaller, until they looked like insects down there, until I could no longer see them, and then we were above the clouds and all I could see were the marshmallowy pillows of cloud beneath us, an occasional plane in the distance on its own journey, and the sun.

I leaned back in my chair and considered my mother making a similar flight as an excited teenager. Had she been as amazed by the experience as I was? Was she excited by the country that waited for her when the plane landed?

And was she looking down now, watching me as I followed in her footsteps?

Mexico City was dark as we descended.

I watched through the window as the city lights grew bigger and brighter, until I could make out the runway. I crossed my fingers that the pilot was very experienced and wouldn't be confused by all of the different lights.

We landed with a bump so small I barely felt it. It was nothing like the impact I'd expected, and I began to giggle as the plane slowed to a halt.

"Alright there, lassie?"

"I can't believe I've actually just been on a flight! Are we really in Mexico?" I asked.

"Well... unless he took a wrong exit somewhere," Cornelius said.

"What? Is that possible?"

"I'm joking! I'm joking! You, Emily Monk, are now in Mexico. Landing at the same airport your mother did. Now, things will have changed of course over the years, but when you leave this airplane, you'll probably feel just like your dear mother did when she arrived here."

I grinned. "I'm so excited."

"She was too. She sent me a postcard, you know, and it was pretty much all exclamation points. I still have it somewhere. I must show it to you."

"I'd love to see it!" I said.

"We didn't come from money, you know. Exotic holidays like this were unusual among the people we knew. Now it seems like young folks are having gap years and ticking off dozens of countries, but that wasn't the world we grew up in. It was a very big thing for her to do."

"I feel really proud of her. For going on the adventure. I'm only here doing it because you arranged it and invited me. And I'm very grateful, and I know I'll have an amazing time. But I wouldn't have dared do this alone," I admitted.

"Remember that feeling, lassie. Remember being proud of her," Uncle Cornelius said.

His words sent a chill down my spine. I'd always be proud of my mum. Nothing could change that. Could it?

There was no time to ask because Cornelius stood up and reached into the overhead compartments for our hand luggage, and we joined the other passengers and filed off the plane.

Back in London, there had been an enclosed tunnel that connected us from the airport to our plane, and I had assumed that would be the case everywhere. But as I reached the plane's door, I realised that there was no tunnel. There were steps leading down from the plane onto the tarmac, and in front of my eyes was Mexico City! Or, at least, the part of Mexico City that was visible from the plane.

It was too dark to make anything out, and it was colder than I expected. I shivered a little as I took in the scene.

"What's the hold up? Keep it moving!" Someone called out from behind me. I turned and saw a young man in a t-shirt and baseball cap glare at me.

"Oh! Sorry!" I said, as I realised that I was the hold up.

"Don't mind him, lassie, some people have no time to stop and smell the daffodils," Uncle Cornelius called from the bottom of the stairs, where he had waited for me.

We filed across the bare tarmac and through a door into the airport terminal.

Aeropuerto Internacional de la Ciudad de Mexico, I whispered as I read the unfamiliar words from a sign. I stayed close to Uncle Cornelius. If he spoke Spanish, he'd never mentioned it to me, but he was the seasoned traveller out of the two of us.

We joined the line for security and I tried to remember whether I knew any Spanish at all. It seemed only right to make an effort, even if I completely made a mess of it.

The line moved slowly but finally it was our turn, and when Uncle Cornelius moved forward to a pleasant-looking man in a security booth, I followed.

"Good evening," Uncle Cornelius said. He hadn't even raised his voice or adopted a bad Spanish accent, which I knew from television was what many English people did when they were abroad without language skills.

"Greetings! Hola amigo, erm, thank you - gracias! - for letting us in your country," I exclaimed, and offered a broad grin.

The airport worker cocked an amused smile at me, then glanced at Uncle C and raised an eyebrow. He addressed Uncle C, not me. "First time?"

"She's very excited to be here," Cornelius confided.

"Ah, I see. Welcome Miss Emily. You can speak English here, everyone does."

"Oh! Phew! Well, that makes things easier!"

"Here are your passports back. Have a pleasant time in Mexico."

"Wait, is that it? Are we really through?" I asked as we left security and followed the signs towards the baggage collection.

"We are well and truly in Mexico, lassie," Cornelius confirmed.

"I can't believe they let us in!" I exclaimed.

"Well, we're hardly criminal masterminds. It's not like we're sneaking in."

"Well, I know, but still... this is amazing! I feel giddy!"

I wasn't sure why that made me feel so exhilarated - I was hardly a criminal mastermind trying to enter the country without permission. But for whatever reason, I felt overcome with excitement. Had my mother felt the same way? Had she made an embarrassing attempt to use broken Spanish, or had she played it cool like Uncle Cornelius? Or had she even taken the time before the trip to learn some Spanish? That was an option that had never occurred to me to do.

"It's 4am!" I exclaimed as I checked my watch.

"Not in Mexico, lassie. It's 8 o'clock. See the time on that sign?"

I followed his gaze and read 20:00, then laughed. "This is so strange! We've travelled back in time!"

"Your body will feel like it's 4am though. That's why I suggested you sleep on the plane."

"I was too excited," I admitted.

Uncle Cornelius beamed at me. "I remember that feeling well. My very first trip abroad, I stayed awake for days! I didn't want to miss a thing. The language, the sights, the sounds... but then, I crashed on day three. Slept for eighteen hours!"

I laughed. "Where did you go?"

"Cardiff," he said, then dived away from me and made a grab for our suitcases. I followed and managed to reach for one case as he tackled the other. With our cases back safe in our possession, we walked out of the baggage claim and down another corridor. Uncle Cornelius definitely led the way as I scurried along beside him.

Little Emily Monk, strolling around a Mexican airport.

If only my mum could see me now.

3

In the pink and white taxi, I practically had my nose pressed to the glass the whole way.

Mexico was out there and I wanted to see every bit of it!

The buildings were low, just one or two storeys high, and they were painted in all the colours of the rainbow.

"They're so pretty!" I exclaimed.

Cornelius and the taxi driver both laughed at me.

The streets were busy and loud with old cars and music coming from roadside cafes and bars. I was definitely an introvert, but the energy of the place was infectious and I was desperate to get out and explore.

As we approached the commercial district, the buildings grew taller and the streets grew even busier.

We pulled up outside the hotel and the taxi driver unloaded our cases from the boot.

"I feel a bit strange," I whispered to Uncle Cornelius.

"Light headed?" He asked.

I nodded.

"We're over 2,000 metres above sea level, lassie. You'll adjust to it. A good night's sleep is what you need."

The hotel was so beautiful, I had the sensation of my breath being taken from me.

There was a huge entrance hall, and a man who stood outside the doors in a beautiful purple suit and dashed to take our suitcases from the taxi. He wheeled them across to the reception desk, then gave me a tip of his hat and returned to his post.

"Can we afford this?" I whispered, although saying we was a creative flourish. I felt it too personal to question whether my uncle's finances could stretch to such beauty.

Cornelius turned and winked at me, then turned his attention to the receptionist, a pretty brunette with blood-red lipstick.

"You're with the Esteban Group, I see," the receptionist purred. Something in her posture straightened a little with that revelation.

"That's right. We were promised a two-room suite," Cornelius said.

"Of course," she said, her cheeks a little flushed. She picked up the phone behind the desk and spoke quietly, in Spanish, into the device.

I wanted to ask what the Esteban Group was, but it could wait.

In fact, I didn't care what claims my uncle had to make, as long as the receptionist found our booking and let us spend a night there. I'd never seen such a beautiful space.

A man appeared by our side; a portly man with an impressive moustache; basically the Mexican version of Uncle Cornelius.

"Welcome! I am Mr Garcia, the owner of this fine establishment. Please, allow me to show you to your suite." He said, then clicked his fingers. A youth sauntered over in the universal way that teenagers have, grabbed our cases, and we filed through the lobby as a group.

Cornelius and the Spanish version of himself chatted, and the youth and I brought up the rear. I tried to think of things to say, but I felt even more shy than was normal for me and so I tuned in to the other conversation instead.

"You have travelled far?"

"We've flown in from London," Cornelius answered.

"Ah, London. I wish to go there. A beautiful city, I think?"

Cornelius nodded with enthusiasm. "Oh, yes. You must visit. It certainly seems that Mexico City is beautiful, too."

"Yes, yes, it is. While you are here, you must see the Basilica de Santa Maria de Guadalupe. It is truly an extraordinary cathedral. I would be happy to arrange a tour for you," Mr Garcia gushed.

"That sounds good. Maybe a day or two for us to settle in and then we can explore a little."

"Of course. As you wish. I'd also recommend a tour of the Teotihuacan pyramids. I can arrange that for you as well. We also have canal trips in Xochimilco available if you don't mind a short trip out of the city. There is no better boat ride in the world! The music, the wildlife... it is amazing! You must go!"

"It sounds wonderful. We'll be sure to do as much as we can to explore this wonderful place!" Cornelius said.

I watched the young porter with interest. How could he appear so at ease in these surroundings? The marble floors, the enormous fountain in the middle of the lobby, complete with a winged baby playing a harp. How could his eyes not be drawn to every crevice and painting? Not to mention the other guests, who all seemed so at ease in their skin as they strolled the lobby in linen tops, pastel shorts and enormous sunglasses.

We rode the elevator for what seemed like no more than a second, but must have been longer as we emerged on the eighteenth floor. The older man opened the door, handed Cornelius the key, and then the two shook hands.

"I will be seeing you at the meeting in a few days," Mr Garcia said.

"You will indeed," Cornelius said.

"If I can do anything at all in the meantime, please let me know. I am here all hours. Nothing is too much trouble, I assure you."

"We certainly appreciate that."

The teenager wheeled in the luggage and left without a word to any of us.

Finally, Cornelius and I were alone.

"There must be a mistake," I breathed as I took in the surroundings.

"Nope," Cornelius grinned.

I took in the view first - the windows were floor to ceiling and opened out on to a wide balcony, complete with sun loungers, a wicker chair and table set, and what looked suspiciously like a hot tub.

"This can't be for us," I insisted.

"Welcome to the finest suite that Mexico City has to offer! Two bedrooms, a lounge, two bathrooms, and a mini bar that isn't that mini. Do you have a preference, Emily?"

I turned and saw him, a different bottle of champagne in each hand. I stifled a laugh. "What are you doing? Don't they bill you as soon as you move any of those things?"

"Relax, there'll be no bill for us here," he said with a wink.

"What do you mean? We're not paying for this?"

His jowls wobbled as he shook his head. He placed one bottle of champagne on the plush settee and popped the other. The foamy liquid escaped and I squealed, then giggled as Cornelius dashed onto the balcony and held the bottle over the side. I wondered if anyone was walking on the pavement far below, if the bubbles were being confused as rainfall.

I joined Cornelius on the balcony and gazed out at the city. It was illuminated by all kinds of lights; lights from inside rooms, streetlights and car headlights down below, even the bright glare of floodlights from a football pitch in the distance. I couldn't wait to see the city in the daylight.

"Please tell me what's happening," I urged.

"We're having the time of our lives, that's what's happening!"

I gave him half a smile. "I may not be a traveller, but I do know that normally people have to pay for their own hotel rooms."

"Can I tell you a secret? I haven't paid for a hotel room since 1975!"

"What?! You're joking? How?"

"All we need to do is spare an hour or two to attend a little presentation. As long as we do that, all of this is completely free."

"Time shares? Is this a time share holiday?" I asked. I'd watched enough TV shows to have heard about these trips, the heavy sales techniques they used to get people to invest money they didn't have in holiday homes that were never quite as appealing as the headlines suggested.

"This one isn't. I've done plenty of those over the years, but they're dying out a bit now. I have to be a bit more creative. But if you know where to look, the opportunities are endless! You wouldn't know it, but our friend Mr Garcia has called an emergency meeting for a few days' time. The hotel's in trouble, not that you'd know by looking. Too much competition from places like AirBnB. The owner's invited a few wealthy investors to attend a strategy meeting."

"What does that mean?"

"It means he hopes everyone present will donate money towards the upkeep of the hotel, of course."

"But we - you - we - are you really wealthy like that?" I asked. I pictured the ramshackle house he lived in, the way some rooms still weren't finished despite him having lived there for decades. If Uncle Cornelius was wealthy enough to invest in a hotel, he'd certainly been hiding it well. He didn't even like to leave a tip.

Cornelius raised a bushy eyebrow and offered me a smile. "I'm in a beautiful country with my favourite niece, I think that makes me rich beyond belief."

"Aww," I said with a smile.

"Have you heard of the Day of the Dead?"

"I think so," I said. The words seemed familiar.

"Dia de Muertos, it's an important time here. It's meant to be the time when the loved ones who have passed are closest to us."

A shiver ran across my spine. "It's a time of mourning?"

"No! Not mourning. Celebration! Food! The attitude towards death seems a lot more positive here than back home, where we try not to speak about the people who have gone before us."

I thought back to my dad's behaviour after my mum's death, and shifted a little on the balls of my feet.

"Do you feel her sometimes?" I asked, my voice barely a whisper.

Cornelius let out a breath and shook his head. "I'd like

to. I'd like some sign that she's forgiven me. Selfish really, but I live in hope."

"I don't know if I want to feel her presence or not. I worry that I'd be scared," I admitted.

"Oh, lassie," Cornelius pulled me in and gripped me in a bear hug.

We stayed there for a long time, holding each other and looking out at the lights of Mexico City.

And then we retired for the night, and slept the sleep of the dead.

4
———

Jet lag somehow resulted in me waking very early, and more than a little confused about where I was. I made a coffee using the fancy machine in the room, and staggered out on to the balcony, where I sat under a blanket and watched the city come alive.

Mexico City by day was an incredible sight. The National Cathedral was next to the hotel, and I could barely take my eyes off the stunning Gothic-inspired architecture. It's two bell towers and central dome pierced the sky and I imagined what it would have been like to have been involved with building it.

A knock at the door around 10am interrupted my daydreaming.

I padded across the suite in bare feet and opened the door to reveal an impossibly tall man, who gave a bow and indicated a trolley that carried several silver domes. His name tag revealed his name to be Luis.

"Can I help?" I asked.

"Good morning, miss. Room service," Luis said. His accent was thicker than the other people we had spoken to since our arrival, and I lost myself in the sing-song lilt of his words before realising what he'd said.

"Oh, no, it's not for us," I said. Cornelius hadn't even woken up yet.

Luis frowned a little, then reached into the pocket of his blazer and unfolded a piece of paper. "Majestica Suite?"

I peered around the door and saw that we were indeed staying in the Majestica Suite. I felt awkward for Luis, who was simply doing his job and would no doubt be embarrassed to disturb me because of an error the kitchen had made.

"It must be a mistake, sorry, we haven't ordered anything," I said with a smile.

"Bring it in, my good man!" Cornelius called from inside the suite. I turned, and there he was, behind me in the doorway.

"Uncle C! Your robe!" I exclaimed.

He looked down and saw that his dressing gown had untied and crept open, revealing his baggy underpants. With an impressive slight of hand he pulled the material tightly around himself.

"Well now! Let's not be shy. There are plenty of women who'd have paid for that sight a few years ago!" He said with a grin.

"This isn't ours, is it?"

"Never turn a good breakfast away, lassie! It's the food of champions," he said, which I realised didn't exactly answer my question.

I stood to one side and the man brought in the trolley and busied himself in setting the table for us. Cornelius and I exchanged glances. He winked at me.

"So, Luis, what do you recommend my niece and I do today? It's our first day here and we want to really get to know the city. None of that tourist nonsense for us, we're natural travellers and we want to get to the heart of a place," Cornelius asked.

Luis' cheeks flushed. "The reception desk will be able to give ideas, sir. They will be able to schedule tours for you."

"Nonsense. The reception desk will recommend the things we want to avoid - the bus tours and the restaurants that serve the version of Mexican food that English people like. We want an authentic experience. Where would *you* suggest we go? In fact, tell me, when you finish work or have a day off, where do you go?"

Luis appeared nervous, and I couldn't blame him. For all he knew, we could be crazy English people planning to stalk him after he'd finished his shift. I felt the desire to interrupt and save him from the conversation, but I was also curious to hear his answer.

"Well, sir, I'm not from Mexico City originally. I don't know this place too well. But tonight is Dia de Muertos. The whole city will be celebrating."

I smiled at the idea of attending a whole city party.

"We were just talking about it last night, would you believe! Emily and I can't wait. There's someone dear to us both who is no longer here. Here's a question for you; where is the best place to experience Dia de Muertos?" Cornelius asked.

Luis puffed with pride at that question. He could barely contain the grin on his face. "Oh, now that's a question I can answer! The only place to experience Dia de Muertos is where I come from. It is perhaps too well known now, so many people join, but really there's nowhere else I could be."

Cornelius nodded with enthusiasm. "Excellent! Excellent! Where is this place?"

Luis' cheeks flushed. "It's a place named Janitzio Island. It's fairly easy to get to. A bus or two, a ferry, that's all."

I looked up at him. It didn't sound easy.

"Fantastic. Just a bus, you say? What time is the bus?" Cornelius asked.

Luis paused before answering. "It's actually two buses and a ferry ride. It's several hours away. The bus leaves at 8pm. But don't worry, the celebration will be incredible here too."

"I don't doubt it!" Cornelius declared.

"Very good! And here's a tip for you. Get some rest today if you can. It's a long night," Luis said as he finished laying the table. The food in front of us looked incredible and my mouth began to water.

"Good man, this looks excellent. We'll see you later, Luis."

"Yes, I'll see you later. Have a good day," Luis said, and he showed himself out of the suite.

The door had only just clicked shut when I leaned over and whispered, "this isn't our breakfast, is it?"

Cornelius laughed. "The good man knocked at our door with bounty for our hungry stomachs. That's how it works when you stay in a suite like this. They know you're hungry before you do!"

"Are you really suggesting that the food magically appeared?"

"I'm saying that guests of a certain calibre shouldn't be troubled with the hassle of having to order their own food," he said with a wink.

I frowned. I had no idea whether to believe him, but whatever the truth was, the food set out on the table looked and smelled delicious. I gave in to the rumbling of my stomach and began to help myself to a little of everything.

"Aren't you excited about tonight? It's going to be quite the adventure! I for one can't wait," Cornelius said, partway through chewing a mouthful of spicy sausage and egg.

"You were serious?" I asked.

"Of course! Janitzio Island is famous for its Day of the Dead festival. I can't believe our luck, meeting Luis and him being gracious enough to give us directions. This will be a holiday to remember, that's for sure!"

"I think he only helped us because he felt a little awkward. He said it's hours away, Uncle C."

"Nonsense! It's rare for a tourist to show an interest in getting off the beaten track. He was probably honoured that we would want to experience things like a local. Not many people do that, you know. Most people just stick to the tourist stuff."

"If you say so," I said, and tucked in to the food on my plate. It had been several hours since I'd last eaten. In fact, it had been on the plane - a tray of food in separate compartments that had reminded me of school lunches. At the time, I'd insisted to Cornelius that each item of food tasted better than anything I'd ever eaten before. Of course, that couldn't have been true. The novelty of being up in the sky - actually in the sky! Eating food! - had clearly caused my taste buds to self destruct.

But the breakfast before me in the Majestica Suite really was an incredible taste sensation.

In fact, it was so good, it had even stopped Uncle Cornelius talking.

UNCLE C'S WORLD WIDE WEB LOG

I'm back, which means we survived the flight and are now tucked in the grandest suite that Mexico City has to offer!

E (or not E) looks like she was born for this life. She has declared the best spot on the balcony to be hers, and she's spent many an hour out there, enjoying the sights and sounds.

It reminds me of my first visit to Spain - my first holiday abroad, proper. I couldn't get enough of the new place and everything seemed so different!

Tonight will blow E's mind, or the mind of whoever she is if she isn't E.

We've been invited to Janitzio Island to experience their Day of the Dead festival! The hotel staff are always recognising us as not being the average tourist.

Oh no, not Uncle C and E (or not E). We will venture off the beaten track and see the real Mexico.

The time is 8pm and the place is the lobby of this grand hotel.

Adventure is out there, and we're going to find it...
Uncle C

5

———

We were not in the lobby at 8pm.

We were in the Majestica Suite, one of us poised ready to leave, the other one of us still soaking in a hot bath.

"We're late!" I called.

I could hear Uncle Cornelius singing in the bathroom, although I couldn't make out the song.

I'd seen how full the bath was, and how high the bubbles rose to, before he closed himself in there and promised he'd be just five minutes. That had been almost an hour ago, and he'd topped the water up at least twice in that time.

"I'll be right out!"

"It's already five past. Should I go down and check when the next bus is?"

"No, no, the 8pm bus won't be there yet. The whole concept of time is different over here, Emily. Pour yourself a drink or something, there's plenty of time."

I smiled and shook my head, moved away from the closed bathroom door and returned to the balcony. I had come to think of it as my spot, and I knew already that I'd miss the view, the constant hustle and bustle of the city below me.

I liked the idea of a place where life was less controlled by the clock, and got myself comfortable while I waited for Uncle C.

I was giddy with excitement at the thought of travelling to Janitzio Island and experiencing Day of the Dead for real. It still didn't seem real that I was abroad, that any of this was happening.

I allowed my body to relax into the comfortable chair, and my thoughts wandered.

It was after eight thirty by the time we arrived in the lobby.

"Now I reckon that Luis would be around here if the bus was almost due, and there's no sign of him! I told you time was more fluid here, we're still early!"

"Okay," I said with a shrug.

We sat down and watched people arrive and leave, the women's heels clacking on the marble floor, the men dressed in linen jackets.

"Can I help?" A uniformed woman asked us with a smile.

"Ah, no, we're all good here, thank you. We're waiting for the bus to Janitzio Island."

"Janitzio Island? There isn't a bus to Janitzio Island," the woman said with hew brow furrowed.

"Oh, no, that's right. There's a bus, then another bus," Cornelius remembered.

"And then a ferry," I added.

The woman smiled. "It's quite the trip, you know. Four hours by bus. I guess you're going for the festival?"

"Apparently, it's the best place to experience it?" I asked.

"Sure, sure, although it's amazing right here in Mexico City too, and without the long journey," the woman said.

"We're very excited. It's going to be a real experience for us!"

"We're excited in a respectful way," I added.

"Of course! Very respectful! In England, people die and the whole thing is so morose. It's going to be a real pleasure - an honour - to see it celebrated. Not death, of course. The life. The person who has died. Celebrating their life. Remembering them!"

"I'm sure you would enjoy it very much. But you've missed the 8pm bus," the woman said. She glanced up at the wall, to the large ornate clock hanging behind our heads.

"What? No! We needed to be on that bus! We just had a, erm, a situation to deal with. We were held up by some, erm, important business to tend to," Cornelius blustered.

"Of course," the woman nodded.

"What do we do now?" Cornelius mumbled, more to himself than anyone else.

"I can recommend a nice restaurant for dinner, over-looking the Zocalo plaza. It has a very good menu."

I swallowed as I remembered Cornelius' insistence that we shouldn't be like the other tourists, experiencing the reception staff's curated version of Mexico.

"Maybe we could still go," I squeaked, barely believing the words I heard myself say.

"Lassie! You read my mind! Luis told us how to get there. We can still go. It's just, what did he say, a bus and..."

"Two buses and a ferry. It's possible, of course," the woman smiled at us.

"Well that's what we'll do then!"

The woman took pity on us and wrote down instructions, her handwriting script so perfect I let out a very geeky gasp when I laid eyes on it. I silently filed a mental reminder to ask how she made the curves of her e and o letters so flawless.

"Thank you," I said.

And then we were off, navigating the busy streets of Mexico City.

With a mix of Cornelius' loud voice and hand gestures, we managed to get on the next bus to Morelia.

The rows of seats were packed with people heading home from work, dressed in uniforms and overalls, but also other tourists like us. Near the front of the bus, a young mother chatted on her phone while her toddler cooed away in a slimline pushchair. I smiled and waved at the cute child, who returned my smile with a gap-toothed grin.

We filed off the bus at Morelia and boarded the next bus to Patzcuaro. This second bus was mainly tourists, chatting excitedly and proudly wearing cameras around their necks.

We arrived at Patzcuaro knowing that we had to catch the ferry, but with no idea where to go to do that.

"Most of our fellow bus passengers are going down there, let's join them," Cornelius suggested. The way he meant was a long and barely lit path with huge trees on either side. It looked spooky, but I had no better ideas.

"There's safety in numbers," I said. My voice wobbled between excitement and nerves. I trusted that a crowd of people couldn't all be walking somewhere dangerous, and I trusted my uncle's travel instincts. With a smile, I started walking.

After a mile's walk, we reached the shore of Lake Patzcuaro.

"This is a very special lake, Emily. The men who fish this lake use a traditional net, butterfly-shaped it is. They're famous throughout Mexico. In fact, their image was adorned on the 50 peso bill for many years," Cornelius said as we looked out at the dark body of water.

"That's amazing. I hope we get to see them," I said.

"I'm sure we will, although tourism has eclipsed fishing as the leading industry in this area," Cornelius said.

"Tourists like us," I said.

"No. No, of course not. We aren't your average tourists, lassie. We're travellers! Adventurers!"

Our fellow travellers had led us to the water's edge and all stopped. It seemed clear that they were waiting for the ferry and making the same journey we were.

I watched with interest as some people sat on the ground. A couple opened backpacks and pulled out sweaters, which I envied. The temperature had dropped cool. Others rolled cigarettes, pulled snacks out of pockets, and several got comfortable and fell asleep.

"Let's see when the ferry's expected," Cornelius said.

He scanned the crowd and finally chose a young man who was awake and not engaged with any other activity - not eating, smoking or talking to anyone else.

"I say, do you speak English?" Cornelius asked as he strode across to the man.

"I do."

"My niece and I, we're waiting for the ferry to Janitzio Island. I guess this is the right place?"

The man gave a small smile and nodded his head. "You and the rest of the world, all waiting for the ferry."

"Thank you. And when would you say the ferry is due?"

With that question, the man laughed and revealed perfectly white teeth. Whoever our new tour guide was, he was a handsome young man with a smile that could win prizes. I felt my cheeks flush and forced myself to look away for a moment, grateful that the dark wouldn't reveal my secrets.

"It will come when it comes," the man said with a shrug of his lean shoulders.

"Well, yes, I've travelled enough to know that that's the truth the world over. I tell you, one time I was waiting for a connecting train at Cambridge, and there were leaves on the line... you can guess the rest of the story, I'm sure? Well, anyway, the blasted thing arrived but it was nearly two hours late! And - here's the killer - no food trolley on it!"

The man looked at Cornelius with a good-natured smile on his face, then offered his hand to us each in turn. "Where are my manners? I'm Jose Lopez."

"You can call me Cornelius."

"I'm Emily," I said with a squeak. A jolt of electricity went through me as I shook Jose's hand, which wasn't helped by the fact that he kept amazing eye contact throughout.

"Your first time here?" He asked.

We both nodded.

"You timed it perfectly. Dia de Muertos is the best time to come. It's a fantastic party," Jose explained.

"Where have you travelled from to be here?" Cornelius asked.

"Ah, no. Janitzio Island is my home. I've been working here at Patzcuaro for a week."

"Ah, a man on the inside! Well, Jose, where should we spend the evening to best experience Dia de Muertos?" Cornelius asked.

"The party takes over the whole island. You can't miss it," he said.

"So we'll just wander the streets?" I asked, eyes wide.

"We'll be perfectly safe, Emily!"

"But what if we get lost?" I asked.

"Actually, I have an idea. You can come to my house and meet my family," he offered.

For some irrational hormone-induced reason, my heart sank at the mention of family. I imagined a beautiful wife and mini versions of Jose, then scolded myself. I was experiencing the world! Now was no time to be distracted by a crush!

"We'd be delighted," Cornelius accepted before I could say a word.

"It's very kind of you, but you don't have to," I said.

"It's my pleasure. It's not every day that I have the chance to welcome new friends into my home. Ah, here comes the ferry now," Jose said.

I peeled my gaze away from him and looked out at the water, where an illuminated ferry made its way through the water towards us.

We boarded with Jose and sat with him. Uncle Cornelius made small talk for most of the short journey while I looked out into the darkness.

There were lights ahead, which I guessed must be from Janitzio Island, and as we got closer I saw a huge shape atop the island.

"What's that?" I asked in panic.

Jose laughed. "That's the statue of Jose Maria Morelos. It stands in the highest and most central point of the island. In daylight, it is a real sight."

"Wow," I said. I continued looking at it, but all I could make out in the darkness was that it was a large stone object that appeared to rise out of the island.

"It stands around 40 metres tall. Very impressive to see," Jose said.

"You're named after him?" I asked.

"Jose is a very common name. I'm named after my grandfather," Jose said with a smile.

"This trip is really turning out swell. Meeting new friends! Seeing new places. It's beginning to rival a little trip I took in 1976. Now, that was a trip," Cornelius said with a resolute nod that made the jowls around his face wobble.

The ferry had pulled ashore and slowed to a stop, and we filed off the boat in turn.

Safely back on land, I was immediately overwhelmed by how busy Janitzio Island was. The streets were packed, and street vendors offered tacos, tamales and Gorditas as we passed them.

We were swallowed into the stream of people walking, all heading in the same direction up towards higher ground.

I looked to my side and saw that Jose was still with us.

He felt me looking and gave me a smile. "It's very busy, right?"

I laughed. "It really is! I'm so glad that you're here to guide us. We'd be lost without you! Where is everyone heading?"

"There is a graveyard at the top of the island. We'll go there and then I'll take you to my house to meet my family. We can eat there. I bet you're hungry."

"A truer word has never been spoken! We're famished and we'd love a home cooked meal," Cornelius said. If he had any awkwardness about accepting such generosity from a stranger, he didn't show it.

We followed everyone else up the steep pathways until we eventually reached the graveyard. I gasped in delight.

The gravestones had been beautifully decorated and families sat out around them, chatting and eating. Altars had been arranged with food, drink and even toys.

"The altars have the favourite things for the departed.

It's a token of remembrance and celebration," Jose explained, seeing me gape at the sight.

"Wow," I said. I wished I could say more, but the experience was so new and overwhelming, all I could do was look.

The whole graveyard seemed to be a sea of marigolds, their bright colours illuminated by the thousands of flickering candles that lit the way.

"And the mourners don't mind us being here?" I asked.

Jose shook his head. "As long as we're respectful. Some tourists can invade the privacy too much, but usually it's fine. This is a celebration, not a mourning."

I thought of my mum and how much it had hurt to lose her. How much it still hurt to have lost her. My dad had never encouraged talking about her after her death, which I understood. He coped in the best way he could. I wondered how different an experience it would have been if we had a more Mexican view of death.

"Please tell us if we do anything that's inappropriate," I said.

"You're doing fine," Jose assured me.

We walked the whole length of the graveyard and time seemed to disappear. I had no idea whether we had been walking for minutes or hours when Cornelius finally clapped his hands together, drawing the attention of me, Jose and everyone else in the near vicinity.

"That's plenty of exploring for me. These knees aren't what they used to be and I didn't get a stomach this shape by skipping meals!"

"Let me take you to my home. Follow me," Jose offered.

We did as he asked and he led us through a maze of winding paths until he gestured to a small, brick house with a white and terracotta facade.

He pushed open the door and the smell of spices greeted us.

"Mama, we have guests," he called as we all entered.

The house was compact with bright orange walls, a patterned throw over a small sofa, and a mongrel dog asleep on the floor.

"Mama, what have I said about bringing this stray into the house?" Jose called, but he bent down and gave the dog a firm scratch behind her ears.

"A stray dog?" I asked.

"She thinks she lives here. Don't you, Miss Lulu? Yes you do!"

A door clicked shut down the hallway and an older woman joined us in the living room. She had dark curls past her shoulders, warm eyes and the same smile as her son.

"Mrs Lopez, a pleasure," Cornelius said with a bow.

I wondered whether I should curtsy, then dismissed the idea. "Thank you so much for welcoming us into your home."

She batted the praise away with a slender hand. "You're welcome here. Please, sit. Dinner is almost ready. And don't tell me about Miss Lulu, Jose. What am I supposed to do if you abandon me for a whole week?"

"Get out and speak to real people?" Jose suggested.

Maria rolled her eyes. "Miss Lulu is better than most people. She listens, gives affection and doesn't judge. Have you been to the graveyard?"

Jose nodded. "Emily and Cornelius have come over for Dia de Muertos. I took them up the hill."

"Busy?"

"Very!" I exclaimed.

"More tourists, I bet?" Maria asked.

Jose shrugged. "You know how it is."

"Now, tell me, how long will you be staying on Janitzio Island?" Maria asked. She had moved into the galley kitchen and was piling food into bowls. Whatever she was preparing, it smelled amazing.

"We don't have a plan. We go where we want and think on our feet," Cornelius said. To my horror, he winked at Maria.

"Cornelius was telling me about the famous fishermen. I'd love to see them," I said.

Maria stopped what she was doing and froze.

Jose grimaced.

"I'm sorry. Was that the wrong thing to say?" I asked.

"Of course not! You'll enjoy seeing them, I'm sure. Here, eat," Maria said. She offered me a bowl of food and I gratefully accepted.

"This is *mole poblano*, it has chicken in. It's one of mama's best recipes," Jose explained.

I took a spoonful of the chicken, bean and sauce mix. "Mm, it's delicious. Thank you!"

"See what you're missing when you wander away from home? I bet you didn't eat this well all week," Maria said.

"Of course I didn't, mama," Jose said.

"This is the food of gods! You must have guests every night with this kind of meal, Maria!" Cornelius complimented her.

"Oh, no, it's been many years since this house had guests," Maria said with a clipped smile.

"I find that hard to believe. A beautiful home, a wonderful family like you," Cornelius complimented them.

Jose let out a small sigh. "Mama keeps herself to herself."

"Ah, well, nothing wrong with that," Cornelius backtracked with a grin, although he was the personification of the exact opposite.

"It's not through choice," Maria said.

I glanced at Jose. There was clearly something big going on, but I didn't want to invade anyone's privacy by asking.

Fortunately, Cornelius had none of my reservations around being tactful.

"Whatever do you mean? Why would an attractive woman like you think like that?"

Maria's cheeks flushed and she gazed down into the bowl of food in her lap. It was clear that she was uncomfortable with kind words.

"It's a long story," Jose said.

"You don't have to tell us," I said.

"It's not that long of a story," Maria said.

He shook his head. "Okay. Well, my father, Daniel, he was a fisherman. He drowned. He just didn't come home one night and the next morning they found his boat. He was tangled in the butterfly net."

"That's awful. I'm so sorry," I said. My heart ached for Jose and his pain of losing a parent.

"You're hiding away in grief? That doesn't seem like the Mexican way," Cornelius said.

"It's not that. Mama has been accused of murdering him. The people here, they refuse to believe his death was really an accident. Some people say it's witchcraft, that mama is a witch and placed a spell on his boat. There are people here who won't meet her gaze, they say to look in her eyes is to be doomed," Jose explained. His voice shook as he spoke and it was clear that he was angry with the way his mother had been treated. I wondered if that was why he spent time away from the island.

"But that's ridiculous. Fishermen have tragic accidents. Why wouldn't people believe that?" I asked.

"Well, for one, my father was the most celebrated fisherman the island had seen in many years. So people just don't believe he could ever have an accident like that. But the other thing is mama's background. She's a nurse, originally from Mexico City, and we don't attend mass very often. The two things together led to rumours before the accident," Jose said.

"These people never accepted me. Daniel's death was the excuse they were always looking for to exclude me," Maria explained.

"That's terrible. Why do you stay?" Cornelius asked.

Maria smiled. "This is my home. I've packed up my life and moved away once. I don't want it again. This island to me is Daniel. Every part of it has a memory of him attached to it. If I leave here, I feel like I'll be leaving him too."

"You're not seeing those memories by staying at home, mama," Jose said what I had been thinking. If Maria was only locking herself in the house, she could do that anywhere.

"Don't you join in with the festival? Everything outside is so beautiful, with the lights and decorations," I said.

Maria shook her head. "We have an altar here. That's all I need."

"Could I see it?" I asked.

"Of course."

Cornelius and I nodded and rose from the chairs.

We followed Maria to the door right off the lounge, and I guessed that it was the room she had been in when we had arrived.

It was a small space, but the whole room was devoted to Daniel Lopez. The altar itself was lit by dozens of candles, and featured photographs of Daniel, marigolds, sugar skulls and various trinkets.

A shudder ran through me.

"This is incredible," I said, and I meant it. I could see the comfort that it would bring to keep him so close. It was almost as if he was in the room.

"Thank you. His actual grave is out there, of course. I wish I could give him a public altar," Maria said.

"You can, surely?" Cornelius said.

"I offer to go with her but mama is scared of what people will say," Jose said.

"Well, there's four of us now. Strength in numbers! They'd have to be very silly indeed to pick an argument with me around. I'm in prize fighting condition, I'll have you know," Cornelius said, and I had probably never loved him more.

"Yes. We can all go!" I agreed.

Cornelius winked at me. "That's the spirit, lassie!"

"I don't know," Maria said. She looked at Jose for his opinion.

"I'll do whatever you want, mama," he said.

She took one last look at the altar, collected a single marigold, and turned back to us. "Okay, okay. Let's go."

As soon as we left the house, it was clear that the people of Janitzio Island were scrutinising us in a way they hadn't when it was just me, Cornelius and Jose.

Several people glanced at us, saw Maria, and averted their gaze. I could feel their disdain. I moved closer and linked my arm through hers, hoping that my action was a universal sign of solidarity.

"Bruja! Bruja!" A young boy screamed as he saw us. He ran back to his mother who tutted at him, but then covered his eyes and closed her own.

I felt Maria stiffen beside me.

"It's just words, mama. We're okay," Jose said.

"Just words! That woman there, Alejandra, she used to barter me for fish. Always promising to pay next week. I wrote off so many debts of hers because I knew how many mouths she had to feed. Now, in my hour of need, where has she been?"

"Idle minds believe idle words, mama," Jose said.

Maria said nothing. Another group of people approached us and I could feel her brace herself for another attack. None came. The group simply looked away, walked by as if we didn't exist. It had been so different when we had walked with Jose earlier - so many people had waved or greeted him.

As we approached the graveyard, a tiny old woman with an occasional tooth in her mouth walked right up and glared at Maria.

"What are you doing with these gringos, Bruja?" the old woman said.

"Josefina, please. We aren't looking for any trouble," Maria said.

"In that case, turn around and go home. And take your tourists with you!" Josefina said.

"Fine. I won't be part of bringing upset to the graveyard," Maria said. She turned on her heels and pushed past us, her shoulders hunched over as she raced to get away from the locals who had turned on her.

"Mama, don't let them win!" Jose called after her, but she was already out of earshot.

6

———

Back in Jose's house, Maria was nowhere in sight but the door to the altar room was closed and we could hear soft cries coming from within.

"This is awful," I said as we awkwardly stood around in the living room.

"It makes me so angry! She doesn't deserve this," Jose said. The anguish was written across his cute face.

"We should, erm, leave you to it. We wouldn't want to overstay our welcome," Cornelius said. His bluster had abandoned him in the face of a woman's tears.

"No, please, it's getting late. There won't be another ferry tonight. You must stay," Jose insisted.

"But we never came expecting to be invited into someone's home. We can find a hotel, maybe, or just keep wandering the streets until daylight. I've done that before. In fact, let me tell you this quick story. It was the summer of 1982, or was it '83? It was the year I was in love with Peggy Foster, I remember that much. I think '82, probably July but it could have been the start of August as I..."

He was silenced - thankfully - by the sound of the altar

door opening. Maria appeared in the lounge doorway, her eyes red and puffy from crying.

"Mama," Jose whispered. He opened his arms and she crossed the room and allowed him to hug her, but even as he did I could see her resolve returning. Her tears had dried and her posture spoke a thousand words.

"Now, we have visitors. Enough of this nonsense. We don't have much, but what we have we will share. You will stay here tonight, yes?" Maria asked.

I glanced at Cornelius, who looked like a rabbit caught in a headlight.

"Of course. It would be an honour," I said. There was no way I could refuse the hospitality of a woman who had just been embarrassed in such an awful way in front of us.

A smile spread across Maria's face and she and Jose busied themselves with changing bedding and preparing cocoa with a touch of chilli.

Maria gave up her small bedroom for me to sleep in, and Jose gave up his own for Cornelius. I assumed that they would find space in the lounge for makeshift beds, but didn't want to ask.

"I'm pretty beat," I said, and it was true. It had been a long and overwhelming evening of travel and new experiences. I also wanted to get out of the lounge so that Maria and Jose could relax in peace.

"Me too! I apologise Jose, I'll tell you the rest of that story another time," Cornelius said.

Jose's panicked expression told me he had forgotten the story already, but he recovered quickly and gave an enthusiastic, "You must! I look forward to it!"

I closed myself into Maria's room and stripped to my vest and underwear. Her room was like another shrine to Daniel, with photographs on the wall and her bedside table.

I lay down on the soft bed, perhaps more grateful for bedtime than I'd ever been before in my life, and my eyes closed instantly.

THE HAMMERING WOKE me up the next day.

It was so loud and insistent that my immediate thought for some reason was that I'd slept in so late, the Lopez family had decided to get on with home renovations in an attempt to wake me.

I dressed quickly, then scampered across to the one bathroom in the house, where I squeezed some toothpaste onto my index finger and used the finger as a toothbrush. I splashed cold water on my face and then undressed, flipped my knickers inside out, and put them back on. It was less than ideal, but I hadn't planned ahead enough to bring a spare pair on the adventure with me.

At some point during that series of strange ablutions, the hammering stopped.

When I left the bathroom, I could see that Jose was at the front door speaking to someone, and I could hear that whoever was there was not happy.

Maybe they hadn't appreciated the DIY either.

I went to his side. "Is everything okay?"

The old woman from last night was shouting at him, the emotion in her voice obvious even if I didn't understand what she was saying.

He looked at me and he seemed impossibly weary. Still cute, but it was clear he was getting towards the end of his tether with the situation, and I couldn't blame him.

Josefina continued to rant from outside the door.

"What's she saying?"

Jose sighed. "She's saying that mama has gone too far now."

I don't know what came over me but I pulled the door open a little wider and gave Josefina my biggest smile. "Look, you have it all wrong. Maria isn't a witch. She's a lovely woman and she wouldn't hurt anyone."

Josefina rolled her eyes at me. "What do you know about it? You tourists understand nothing. You come and you go. The she-witch was furious last night! I angered her and I was punished for it."

"What do you mean?" Jose asked.

"Bring her out here and let her tell you! It's time you learned who your mama really is!"

Jose rubbed the bridge of his nose and let out a sigh. "There's no reasoning with this madness."

"I'll speak to her," Maria's voice came from behind us. Jose and I both turned and looked at her. She looked incredibly fresh to say she had cried so much last night and then slept on a chair.

"You don't have to. No good can come of it," Jose protested.

"This isn't your trouble to bear," Maria said.

Jose obediently moved away from the door and I did the same, although we both stayed close.

As soon as Maria appeared in the doorway, Josefina hissed at her, and then her anger crumbled in front of her eyes and she started to sob.

"How could you? How could you do this?" Josefina managed to choke out in between sobs.

A chill ran through me.

This wasn't about Daniel.

"What's happened?" Maria asked, clearly reaching the same conclusion as me.

"You know what happened! She-witch, you did it! We know what, but why? Tell me why? Because I dared to challenge you last night? Come for me, you monster! Come for me!"

"Josefina, what's happened?" Jose asked.

The old woman crumpled to the floor and began to pummel the ground with her fists. It was a pitiful sight and I felt my heart go out to her, even though she had been awful to Maria.

Unbelievably, it was Cornelius who saved the moment. He barged past Maria and sat on the ground next to Josefina, where he placed a cup of tea in front of her and began an awkward rubbing of her hunched back.

"There, there. Let it all out," he soothed.

Josefina eyed him warily and didn't touch the drink. "What is this? This isn't coffee."

"Oh no, it's a good old cup of tea. I never leave home without a few in my trouser pocket. A cup of tea solves everything!"

"I don't trust any drinks made in the witch's house!"

Maria scoffed from the doorway. "Josefina, you babysat Jose for me. You've known me for many years. How can you believe these things?"

"I have more proof than ever today. You cannot deny it any longer!" Josefina shouted from the ground.

"What do you mean?" Jose asked.

"She doesn't have the courage to say it, so I shall have to! The she-witch has taken another life! I angered her and she punished me. She punished me with the death of my son," Josefina wailed.

"What?" I asked.

"Francisco?" Jose mouthed.

"Lord, say it isn't true," Maria whispered. She moved

from the doorway and dropped to the ground herself, but Josefina blocked any efforts Maria made to touch her.

I watched Maria's primal instinct to comfort her grieving enemy and thought she was a better woman than many.

"Say it isn't true," Maria repeated, but it was unclear who she was speaking to.

"Tell us what happened?" Jose asked.

"You know what happened! The she-witch was angered. Francisco went out fishing last night and his body was found this morning, just as she did to Daniel. My son, Maria Lopez! My son! How could you?"

"I...I..." Maria stammered.

"Even after what you did to your husband, I say hello to Jose. I do not punish the son for the mother's crimes!"

"I... but..."

"Admit it! If you are monster enough to do these terrible things, be brave enough to admit them!" Josefina shouted.

"I didn't do it," Maria said. Her voice was tiny, as if she herself was doubting the truth of her words, or had no confidence to say them out loud.

"I do not know why I wasted my time to come and speak to you. Next time, take me. I have nothing. I have nothing to live for now," Josefina said as she pushed herself up from the ground.

She took a long, hard look at each of us, and in her deeply wrinkled face, I saw nothing but sorrow. With a sad shake of her head, she turned and began a slow walk away.

We remained there, outside the house, for some time, each of us in shock.

"Do you think she's telling the truth?" Jose broke the silence.

"Death is not a thing you lie about," Maria said. Her eyes were dull and while her body was with us, her spirit was elsewhere. No doubt Josefina's grief had made her relive Daniel's death.

"Come on inside, let me make everyone something to eat," Cornelius said.

We all trailed after him back into the house, where the colours seemed muted.

Maria collapsed into a chair and Miss Lulu, who had managed to sneak back in while the door was open, jumped on to her knee. Jose didn't utter a word against it.

"How about I make eggs for us all?" Cornelius offered.

Maria didn't answer but Jose gave a thumbs up.

"I'll help," I said.

I joined Cornelius in the kitchen area, where he promptly took on the role of supervisor and left me to prepare the breakfast.

"What do you think will happen to Maria now?" I whispered, aware that our voices could carry into the adjoined living room.

"She'll be even more of an outcast than before, that much is clear. The poor woman."

"Do you think the police might investigate?"

Cornelius' face blanched. "I hadn't thought of that. I guess they could."

"Surely we can give her an alibi for last night?"

He shook his head. "We were asleep. Or at least, I was. That kind of alibi is useless. We weren't even in the same room, and she was closer to the door."

"And I'm scared that with the whole island against her, she might not be treated fairly by the authorities," I muttered as I poured the eggs into a hot pan.

"Lassie, I can see those cogs working. You're planning to investigate, aren't you?" Cornelius said with a grin.

"No!" I objected. I was actually just planning on

enjoying a holiday, not getting wrapped up in a murder case. But then I thought of Maria's hospitality, the way she had welcomed us into her home without hesitation, even after suffering so much unkindness from other people.

"Of course you're not," Cornelius teased.

"I just think... I... maybe we should look into things," I said.

We were interrupted by a single bang on the door. I turned in time to see Jose pick up a piece of paper that had been pushed underneath the door.

"What is it?" I asked.

He held up the flyer for us all to see. "Island meeting this morning. Everyone must attend."

"Is that a regular thing?" Cornelius asked.

"No, it most definitely isn't. This is bad news," Jose said.

"Maybe they want to make an announcement about Francisco's death? Advise everyone to be careful when fishing?" I suggested.

"Maybe," Jose said, but it was clear he wasn't convinced.

"Well, we shall go to this meeting together. It's the least we can do. After I finish these eggs, of course!" Cornelius exclaimed, although he made no effort to take over the egg-making from me.

7

———

The island meeting was held in the open air theatre, the only space big enough to fit everyone who had turned out.

"Now we know this is serious. This space should be full of the dancers for the festival all day today," Jose explained as we swarmed into the space along with crowds of people.

Maria had covered her head with a shawl and when we took seats, she allowed me and Cornelius to sit in between her and Jose. Her nerves were palpable.

I watched with interest as a white man in a suit, with a Stetson atop his head, sauntered across to the small podium that had been erected.

"Howdy there, folks. We meet on an awful sad day," he said with a Texan accent, and the mention of Francisco's death encouraged the crowd to fall into a hush.

"Who is he?" I asked.

Jose shrugged his lean shoulders and I thought that shoulders had never looked so lean. He was a man who made shoulders look good.

"Many of you will now have heard about the tragic death

of one of our own, Mr Francisco Martinez. Now, I didn't know Francisco personally but I've been to San Francisco a few times and I'm sure the man was as great as the place," the American said, with about as much cultural tact as a steamroller.

"And to think that I used to consider myself a little tactless," Cornelius said without lowering his voice.

"Forgive me, I'll introduce myself. I'm Bradley Hart, and you may have noticed the twang of an accent. I'm from the good old USA, here purely for vacation, but I do have the advantage of a long line of fishing as my business. I've made a heck of a lot of money, in fact, from fishing. Now, when I came here, I saw your butterfly fishermen and I thought to myself, 'now heck that looks mighty cute, but inefficient'. You know what I'm saying?"

The crowd appeared to have no idea what he was saying, and neither did I.

"How has an American holidaymaker managed to get the whole island here for a meeting?" I whispered to Jose.

"I dread to think. Something is wrong here," Jose murmured back in my ear.

"Now, you might imagine that while on holiday, I should have just been sightseeing and enjoying myself, but I'm a generous guy and if I see a problem, I like to solve it. Or at least try to," Bradley continued.

"What problem are you talking about?" Someone in the crowd called out.

"I'm sure glad you asked! The problem, I don't mind sharing with you, was fishing in a way that limited how rich you could be. I'm happy to share that I am a wealthy man. And once I saw what y'all were doin', I felt it was my duty to share with your leaders here how I became wealthy and how the fine folks of Janitzia Island might do the same."

"He can't even remember the name of the place correctly," Jose tutted.

"I'd already had some interesting - very interesting - conversations with some of y'all and I think we'd really seen eye to eye about the future of commercial fishing. Now that's great news for you, of course, but changes like that take time. Nothing was going to change quickly. And today we learn that a dear friend has met his death in a butterfly net."

"This is making no sense," I mumbled.

"Can we honestly continue the changes at the normal pace, knowing that with each new day more lives may be at risk? Of course not. I've gladly agreed to extend my vacation so that we can get these dangerous practices completely replaced with modern day commercial fishing within the next month. I know, y'all will want to thank me, but my ego won't allow all of those kind words, so let's just move to questions."

"He's a politician. He must be. He's spoken for minutes without actually saying anything. I once get entangled with one of those silver tongued sharks for two days straight before I could get him to commit to one side or the other," Cornelius exclaimed.

"My son was killed by the witch," Josefina called out. Many people in the crowd cheered or clapped to support her.

Bradley laughed. "Now that right there is a curious thing to believe. We have two recent deaths in the same manner, and there's nothing magic about it. I can assure you of that. Like I said, the problem is, these nets are dangerous. These boats are ill-equipped. These boats are inefficient death traps. But the changes I'm proposing will make the water safe again. Not to mention put a lot of money in your pockets! You like money, right? Right?"

Cornelius nudged me. I glanced down to see that he had done an online search into Bradley Hart. I scanned the information quickly.

"CEO of Hart Commercial, a Fortune 500 company specialising in commercial fishing boats and shipping containers," I read aloud.

"He's making great pains on this site to show that he knows his way around a boat, but I bet he'll be overseeing it all from some plush office," Cornelius said with a sneer.

I sighed. "But maybe he has a point. If Maria didn't kill Daniel and Francisco, and we know she didn't, then the alternative is that they both died in fishing accidents. Maybe he can make the waters safer for these people."

"You could be right, lassie. Let's hope so," Cornelius agreed.

"The butterfly fishing is what we are known for," someone else called out.

"I understand and I hear you. It's hard to let go of traditions. But, think long and hard on this one, would you rather be famous and dead, or unknown and alive?" Bradley asked without as much as a pause. He was smooth, I'd give him that.

Maybe his involvement was a good thing for Janitzio Island.

FOR THE REST of the day, Jose insisted on giving us a tour of the island. We trekked up to see the statue of Jose Maria Morelos in daylight and it was an incredible sight, standing so high above everything else on the island.

Cornelius and I posed for photographs, knowing that we looked like cliche tourists by doing so, but not caring.

"How are you feeling?" I asked Jose as we sat down for a rest near the statue.

"I don't even know anymore. It hurts me to see mama living like this, staying at home while we come out, being cast off by the people she has known for years. I wish she would agree to move away with me," he said.

"Do you think the fishing changes could be good for her? Maybe if they do make the accidents stop, it will be clear that they were accidents and people will change their opinion?"

He shrugged. "Even if that happens, how can she rebuild relationships after this? At the time she most needed these people, they abandoned her. I don't think I could ever forgive such a thing."

"No, it wouldn't be easy," I agreed.

Cornelius had continued taking more photographs on his high-spec mobile phone, and he sauntered back across to us with a grin on his face.

"This place really is incredible," he said.

"You'll stay another night?" Jose asked.

"Oh, we'd hate to overstay our welcome," I said, although I was in no rush to leave Jose and Maria, and we had no set date we had to return to Mexico City for.

"That could never happen," Jose said with a smile.

"What do you think, Uncle C?"

"Lassie, I can't think of a single reason why we'd leave today," he said.

With that decided, and with me in a mild panic about how I could re-use my knickers for a third day, we all began the trudge back to Jose's home.

We heard the chanting before we saw the crowd. We could see it when it was still a street away, but it was only as we got closer that we realised what the mass of people were saying.

"Bru-ja! Bru-ja! Bru-ja!"

"What does it mean?" I asked Jose.

"Witch," he said.

The situation came into focus in slow motion, with me realising later than I should have that the people were surrounding Jose's house. Faces pinched in anger, some had brought tools and weapons.

"It's like a witch-hunt," I whispered as we quickly approached.

"What is this? What are you thinking? My mother did not hurt Francisco!" Jose screamed at the crowd.

"We are here to demand justice for Daniel, Francisco and Miguel!"

"Miguel?" Jose asked.

A young woman with long dark hair in a thick plait stepped forward from the crowd. She held a photograph of a man around her age and thrust it towards us. "My brother, Miguel Sanchez. You played ball with him back in the day, Jose."

"I saw Miguel at the festival just yesterday!" Jose said, his voice cracked with a premonition.

"And they just brought his body back in from the water," the sister said.

"No, it cannot be true."

"Trust me, even after the fishes had enjoyed him, I still recognised the man I shared a womb with," the sister spat.

"It can't be right. I need to speak to mama. You all have homes, go away! Leave us alone!" Jose said.

He unlocked the door and we all entered and locked the door behind us.

We found Maria on the settee, her head under a cushion.

"Mama?" Jose asked. There was no response. He called her again, louder and louder, but she didn't move.

Fearing the worst, I moved forward and gave Maria a soft shake.

She stirred immediately, and I saw that she had headphones in, the volume so loud I could hear the beat of the music as soon as the cushion was moved.

She looked frantically between us. "Are they still out there?"

Jose nodded. "I've told them to move on. They say that Miguel has died."

Maria nodded. "What is happening? So many deaths. I'm starting to believe that I am causing them somehow."

"You don't believe they're all accidents?" I asked.

"Our waters are safe, our fishermen are skilled. Every fishing community has its share of grief and accidents, but not like this. Not so many. Last night and now today as well? Maybe I am a witch."

"You know that's not true. Even if you were a witch, why would you want those people dead? Your own husband? These men you knew, it would make no sense," I argued.

"She's right, mama."

"But they all believe it is me," Maria said.

"It's going to be okay," Jose soothed.

Maria let out a harsh laugh. "How?"

"We'll move away. I have opportunities, mama. You can start over," Jose urged.

"No. I refuse to run away like this. I may have no reason to still be proud, but I am. I'm a proud woman, and I won't be pushed away from my home," Maria said. It was clear that there would be no persuading her otherwise.

"Let us help you," I said.

"Help us how?"

"We have a little experience, don't we lassie? We can investigate what's happened and get to the bottom of things," Cornelius explained.

"Exactly," I agreed.

"But the bottom of things is that three fishermen have died in tragic accidents," Jose said.

"Maybe. And if that's the case, maybe we can find proof to show everyone that that's the case. But I think that three deaths so close together is starting to stretch things a bit too far," I said.

"What does that mean?"

"It means we might be dealing with murders after all, and we have to find out who the real killer is so we can clear Maria's name," I said.

A silence fell on the room as the gravity of my words sank in.

Murders.

Investigation.

I had no evidence to support my hunch, but I knew that there was something fishy going on here. No pun intended.

8

———

"Where would you start?" Maria asked.

"I'd need to get an understanding about the men who died. I don't know any of them. It would make sense to start with Daniel. Could you tell me about him?" I asked.

"Of course, I knew him better than I know myself," Maria agreed.

I nodded.

"What do you want to know?"

"Anything you like. Paint me a picture of him with your words," I encouraged.

Maria looked up and became lost in memories. "He was kind. The kindest man I ever knew. It is where Jose saw how to be a man, so you look at Jose and you can imagine how good a man Daniel was."

"I certainly can," I said, with a smile to Jose. His cheeks flushed at the compliment.

"He was a fisherman. He lived for the water. He was never really at home on land. His heart ached for the water. Always on that boat, it was the only thing we ever argued about, especially when Jose was a baby. I wanted Daniel home with us more and Daniel needed to be out on the water. He had to catch the fish to make a living, that's true."

"He was good at fishing."

"He was the best. You can ask anyone. Even though they hate me, everyone in town would tell you. They only hate me because they were so sad to lose him. He was good and quick and careful too, the safest of fishermen. He never took risks in bad weather. He never overloaded the boat. He took no shortcuts, because he always wanted to make it home to us."

"Of course he did. Was there anything different about the night he died?"

Maria considered the question for a moment then shook her head. "It was a normal night. I don't even remember him leaving clearly. I can't remember if I kissed him goodbye. I must have been busy with some foolish tidying, distracted from the last moments with my husband. How terrible is that?"

"We all do it, love," Cornelius soothed.

"I went to bed and I woke up early. He wasn't home but that wasn't unusual. I got on with my morning. At some point the message came and the rumours had started that same day."

"That's awful," I said.

"Had the weather been bad?" Cornelius asked.

"I don't know. I was asleep. I don't think there were any storms, but the weather on land isn't a sign of the water conditions. It could have been fine here and different there."

"Was the boat damaged?" I asked.

Maria frowned. "I don't know. I never asked that question."

"Even if it was, that wouldn't mean much. The boat

wasn't anchored, so it was moving through the water on its own as soon as dad fell. It could have just strayed onto the rocks," Jose explained.

"Okay, that makes sense. And Daniel was actually in the net? I'm sorry to have to be so detailed," I cringed.

My words caused Maria obvious pain. She slumped over in the chair and began to cry.

"Yes, he was tangled in the net. It's the biggest risk to fishermen here, but it isn't something that happens often," Jose had taken over the talking.

"And there was no reason why he might have been distracted on that night?"

"Oh!" Maria exclaimed. She looked up at me with damp eyes.

"You remember something?" I asked.

"I'd forgotten completely. I was unwell that night, that's why I don't remember much about before he left. I had a temperature. It had cleared by the morning."

"But it could have been on his mind?"

"I guess," Maria said.

"That's interesting."

"But please remember, he had been on those waters while I was pregnant, he was out there when I was almost due, and then he was leaving me and a tiny baby. He couldn't only fish when there was nothing else on his mind."

"Of course," I said.

"Did you have any contact with him while he was fishing? Did he have a radio out there or anything?" Cornelius asked.

Maria shook her head. "He didn't want the distraction. He always said if he had an emergency out there, calling for help on the radio would do no good as help couldn't reach him quick enough. When he was on that boat, he was unreachable."

"Did he have any enemies?" I asked.

Maria's head moved quickly and her eyes met mine. "What are you saying? Someone hurt him?"

"No, but we have to consider all options. Could anyone have wanted to hurt him?"

Maria scoffed. "Like who? A jealous fisherman? Everyone who knew him loved him."

"Well, this is helpful," Cornelius said with a smile.

I knew him well enough to hear that the sentiment wasn't sincere. I'd ran out of questions and was no further forward in terms of understanding what had happened.

A popular man alone on a fishing boat with no way to call for help? It seemed obvious that his death had been a tragic accident.

But a tragic accident that had repeated itself twice more since our arrival yesterday?

Surely that couldn't be the case.

And if it was, perhaps Bradley Hart's plan for the fishing community was the best news that Janitzio Island could hope for.

"What do you think about Bradley Hart?" I asked.

Maria rolled her eyes. "Another American businessman who sees opportunity here, of course. Using our grief for his own benefit. That story he told today? Nonsense! He was in a suit! Who travels on holiday in a suit?"

I cast my mind back and pictured Bradley Hart, suit and Stetson, addressing the island's people as if it was just another business meeting.

Then I considered my own kind of travel wardrobe. I hadn't even packed a change of underwear, never mind a full suit.

HE LEAD us through the winding streets of Janitzio Island with Miss Lulu trailing at his heel, until he indicated towards a small home. The dusty path was covered with marigolds, and we could hear the wailing inside before we even reached the door.

Jose rapped on the door and we heard shuffling from within. He was confident that Josefina would speak to us, as long as Maria wasn't with us.

"What is it?" Josefina asked. She eyed Cornelius and I warily.

"Can we come in, *madrecita*?"

"No! Go away!"

"My friends here want to speak with you. They want to help you," Jose explained.

Josefina looked up at us with a scowl. "What help can tourists be to me?"

"We think we can find out the truth of what happened to Francisco, if you'd let us try," I said.

"I know the truth," she called.

"I understand. And if you are right, then we will help you prove it. We just want Francisco to have justice," I said, offering a gentle smile.

At her son's name, Josefina began to wail again. She returned to the darkness of the house and left the door open. Jose shrugged and lead us inside.

We followed Josefina to a modest lounge, where she sat in a wicker chair.

But she wasn't alone.

I recognised him by the Stetson, of course.

"Ah, you have more friends to visit. I'll be on my way. Now remember what I said, Mrs Martinez. Your son's death will not be in vain," Bradley Hart said in his thick drawl as he rose from his chair. He tipped his hat at us on his way out.

"What did he want?" Jose asked.

"He came to pass on his condolences," the old woman said. She reached for the side table and picked up a photograph, ran a finger across the glass and smiled a smile of longing.

"Of course. We're very sorry for your loss," Cornelius said as he shifted on his feet.

"You stay with the she-witch who did it! Have you seen sense now? Realised that she is evil?" Josefina asked.

"Mrs Martinez, we're looking into all of the deaths. Francisco's, and Miguel and Daniel too," I explained.

"So you see that they weren't accidents?"

I crossed the room in a few steps and sat on the floor in front of Josefina. "I don't know yet. But I'd like to find out. Can you tell me about your son?"

Josefina turned the photograph around so that I could see. The man in the picture must have been in his 50s, meaning Josefina had been a young mum. She had spent most of her life with Francisco by her side. His death would be devastating for her.

He looked out from the image, forever frozen in time, standing aboard a boat. He hadn't realised the image was being taken. He didn't look at the camera and he didn't smile. He was working, doing something with the butterfly net that had been his downfall, his bare arms tanned and muscular from days of hard work.

"He was a good son," Josefina said with a shrug.

"What was he like?"

"He was like the man who always had time for his mother. I needed shopping, he helped. I felt ill, he fetched the doctor. I needed to eat, he'd catch the fish. For many years now it has been him and me."

"He sounds like a wonderful man. Being a fisherman, that was his job?"

"Of course," Josefina said, as if the question was stupid. Maybe it was. Maybe this was a place where the waters were reserved for work, not pleasure.

"And he was good at his job?" Cornelius asked.

"Oh! Here it comes! This is where you try to say that he was not paying attention, or fell asleep, or drunk? Not my Francisco! He was a hard worker!"

"Forgive us. We have to ask," I urged.

"How about enemies? Did he have any fall outs, anyone he didn't get along with?" Cornelius asked.

"These questions! I know the truth, it was the she-witch!"

"We're trying to help," Jose encouraged.

"Fine! Fine! He had to let go of the young man who helped him. Now there was a fisherman who was lazy. I know he was a friend to you, Jose, but it's the truth. For many days, Miguel didn't arrive for work. Other days he came but so late Francisco had left without him."

"Miguel? Really?" Jose asked.

"I know he was a friend to you. He wasn't a bad boy, not really, he just wanted to be young. Francisco gave him chance after chance and then told him enough is enough."

"And this is the same Miguel who has also died?" I clarified.

Josefina nodded her head.

"That's interesting. Do you know how Miguel reacted when Francisco let him go?"

"He was angry, of course. His pride was hurt. Young men

like that, it's all the pride. He made some threats but it wasn't serious."

"He threatened Francisco? To hurt him?"

"To throw him overboard and feed him to the fish. So dramatic! As if he could have laid a finger on my beautiful Francisco. My son was strong! It was all funny, really," Josefina said with a shake of her head.

"But that's what did happen to Francisco," I muttered.

"Are you thinking what I am, lassie?" Cornelius asked.

"Miguel could have killed Francisco and then hurt himself because of the guilt?" I asked.

"Miguel wouldn't do that," Jose said.

"No? You knew him well enough to vouch for him?" I asked.

"Well, I thought I knew him well. We played ball and hung out. He liked to live a pretty low key life. I can believe that he'd not be the hardest worker, but to hurt another person? No way," Jose said.

"He didn't have a temper?" Cornelius asked. His eyebrows darted up his head, like a crazed caterpillar dancing.

Jose shook his head. "Not enough to kill someone. Sure, he could shout if he missed a goal but so could I. He wasn't a killer."

"I agree," Josefina said.

"Okay," I said.

We sat in silence for a few moments, Josefina's shaky breath the only noise in the room with us. I knew that murderous rages could affect the people we would least suspect.

Sometimes, all it took was one last disappointment or slight, just one more bad day in a series of bad days, and a normally placid person could snap.

I also knew that those murderous rages passed, but the damage done lasted forever. How could a good person live with the guilt of having done an awful thing?

I had to listen to what these people said about the type of person Miguel was, but I also realised that it was very likely he had killed Francisco, regretted it immediately, and paid with his own life.

"Where can we find Miguel's family?" I asked, as I patted Josefina's knee and got back up to my feet.

9

Miguel's parents lived right by the water, in the biggest home we'd seen since arriving on Janitzio Island.

It was his father, Antonio, who opened the door to Jose's knock. Antonio was a man in his early 40s, with leathered skin and a thick moustache. Jose had told us that he worked for local government. His wife, Donna, was a secretary in the government buildings too. Miguel had been their only son, born after years of rumours that the couple couldn't conceive.

"Jose, son," Antonio greeted, his voice thick with emotion but his eyes dry. He pulled Jose in for an embrace and slapped him on the back harder than his slender body would suggest he was capable of.

"I bring friends, *papi*. Can we come in?"

"Of course, of course," Antonio said. We followed him into a kitchen diner and sat around a formica table.

"Donna!" Antonio called.

His pretty wife appeared within seconds, her hair

pinned back. She wore a plain dress and an apron and immediately filled the kettle.

"So sorry, I was just freshening up," she apologised, her voice thick with un-cried tears.

"I'm so sorry," Jose said. He rose from his chair and gave her a hug, a much more gentle affair than his embrace with Antonio. Donna allowed herself to sink in to him, and we all averted our eyes as she showed no eagerness to pull away.

Eventually, Antonio cleared his throat, and Donna pulled back, her cheeks flushed. "Sorry, sorry. I closed my eyes and... and you're so like him. Both big, strong boys. I just let myself dream for a moment that you were him."

"It's okay, *mami*," Jose said. He seemed strangely at ease around grief and I wondered if that was because his culture had such a different view of death, or because he had lived through it by losing his dad.

I'd lost my mum but remained awkward around other mourners.

"You'll embarrass the boy," Antonio scolded his wife with a wink.

"Never. How are you both doing?"

Antonio shrugged as the kettle boiled and Donna busied herself with making drinks for us all.

"It is difficult. But I know he is with our Lord. When I start to cry, I remember that he is in a better place now," Antonio said.

Donna returned to the table and handed strong coffees out to us all.

There were only four seats at the table and she remained standing and hovered at the end.

"Have my seat," Jose sprung out of his chair.

"No, no. I prefer to stand," Donna said.

Jose sat back down and cupped the drink in his hands.

"My friends here, they're looking into what happened to Miguel. And Francisco. My dad too. They want to ask you a few questions."

"We've already spoken with the police," Antonio asked.

"We're more like private investigators," Cornelius said with a twinkle of mischief in his eyes.

"Well, I'm not sure if we should speak to you," Antonio continued.

Donna reached out and touched his arm. "Jose wouldn't ask us to do anything we shouldn't."

Antonio sighed. "Fetch me a pen and paper, Donna. I may need to take notes."

Donna left the room and Antonio leaned in and studied the three of us. "I have your word that you're not asking me to do something I'll regret?"

I swallowed as I considered the very real possibility that our investigation might reveal his son to be a murderer.

"We are searching for the truth. As long as you have no objections with the truth being found, you won't regret it," I said, choosing my words carefully.

Donna returned with a spiral pad and an expensive-looking fountain pen, which Antonio laid out in front of him on the table.

"Well, it has to be better than the nonsense that Maria Lopez is a witch," Antonio muttered.

"You don't believe that?" I asked.

Antonio scoffed. "Of course we don't. Even if she was a witch, she wouldn't have hurt her husband. She was a good wife, she took care of him well. She raised a good son here, as you know. I take it you don't believe these rumours also?"

"That's the reason my niece here and I decided to take on this case. Although I'm not so sure on witchcraft generally, I'm man enough to admit that. I was at a stately home one November and I had the strangest thing happen. I walked into one of the rooms and there was a real chill. It came on from nowhere, I tell you. And I got out of that room pretty quick! There was something in there that didn't want me intruding," Cornelius said. I shot a glance at him. This was a story I hadn't heard before.

"November *is* chilly in your country, no?" Antonio asked.

"Well, yes, yes, of course, but this was a different kind of chill. Not your average November chill. So there was the November chill and that was in every room I went in, but this particular room, there was a blast of frigid air right away and the feeling that I was most unwelcome!"

"I see," Antonio said.

"Leave him. I believe there are many things that our educated minds cannot explain and it doesn't make them any less real," Donna said with an encouraging smile to Cornelius.

"Perhaps," Antonio said, then returned his attention to us. "My wife here has a more open mind about things like that. But one thing we agree on is that Maria Lopez was not responsible for anybody's death."

"The way she is treated now is terrible," Donna said with an enthusiastic nod.

"Can you tell us a bit about Miguel? Jose has told us some things but it would be good to hear from you too," I asked.

"We can talk all day about him. But to give you information that might be helpful? He was young for his age. A little irresponsible."

"Don't talk about him like that," Donna scolded.

"I'm just telling the truth," Antonio said with a shrug.

"Miguel was a good boy. He dreamed of being a footballer. Jose knows that, of course. It was his big dream but he had no second choice. He thought to have a Plan B would be admitting failure. So he loved to play ball, he loved chatting with his friends, he liked a pretty girl to look at, and he was always eating! That boy! I couldn't fill him!" Donna said. She laughed as she recounted her son, and Antonio reached across and squeezed her hand.

"He sounds like a big character," I said.

"He was. A big character on a small island. He struggled with that at times. He fought against it. He was always looking for something bigger - more fun, more adventure. I told him he had to start growing up, thinking about responsibility, but what boy wants to hear that?"

Cornelius smiled to himself. "He sounds like me as a younger man."

"You mentioned him liking the ladies. Did he have a girl-friend?" I asked.

Antonio rolled his eyes. "He was in love with a different girl each week. All a girl had to do was walk by him in the street and smile at him, and he was besotted."

Donna laughed. "That's true."

"Did he date?" I asked.

"Not really. Miguel always felt that some magical chance would appear and whisk him away at a moment's notice. It made him reluctant to live his life here. He was waiting for his real life to begin. Plus, he told Donna he would only settle down with a woman as beautiful as she was, and he hadn't found any yet," Antonio's voice beamed with pride.

I looked at Donna. She was attractive in a homely way and it was wonderful to see that her husband and her son regarded her so highly.

"He told me that all the time," Jose said with a smile.

"So there's no chance of any women - any girls - being upset with him? He hasn't broken any hearts?" I asked.

"Goodness, no. He was a gentleman."

"Okay. How did he end up working for Francisco?" I asked.

"He turned 21 and we told him he had to find some work or I was going to kick him out. Dreams are one thing, but a man needs to be able to support a family. So he went to talk to his friends and Francisco offered him a day's work. It went from there," Antonio said.

"Did Miguel enjoy it?"

"He liked Francisco a lot, but I think he found the work dull. He had never dreamed of being a fisherman. In the end, Francisco let him go," Donna explained.

"Do you know why?"

"We didn't pry, but we expect that Francisco had his reasons. I'll say... I was not surprised," Antonio said with a small nod of his head.

"There you go again!" Donna exclaimed.

"It's the truth," Antonio said.

"So, there were no hard feelings towards Francisco for doing that?"

"Not from us. I can't imagine that Miguel would have been too disappointed either," Donna said.

"Would it not have hurt his pride to lose a job?" I pushed, remembering Josefina telling us about Miguel threatening her son.

Antonio frowned. "In some young men, that would be a concern, yes. But not Miguel. He was only doing it because I forced him to. He would much rather have been outside practicing for the next tryout."

"I have a question. If he'd lost his job, why was he even out on the water that day?" Jose asked.

I stared at him. It was such an obvious question and yet it hadn't occurred to me.

"We don't know. He was never allowed on the water alone when he worked for Francisco. He was a helper, not a fisherman."

"That's very interesting. Which boat was he on?" I asked.

Antonio shifted in his seat and then looked at Jose. "You don't know?"

Jose stiffened beside me and shook his head.

"It was your father's boat."

A chill ran through me as I took that information on board.

"You're saying that Miguel was found on Daniel's old boat?" I asked.

Donna nodded. "We don't know what that means, but it must mean something?"

"It could well do. But who does that boat belong to now? Who would be responsible for it?"

Jose swallowed and I knew the answer before he spoke. "The boat is mine."

"Yours?" Cornelius barked in surprise.

"At least in theory. It became mine when dad died. But how could I want the thing that caused his death? It's not been used since his death, to my knowledge at least," Jose explained.

"I can understand that," I said.

"The boat is cursed," Donna murmured.

"Do you really believe that?" I asked.

"No, we don't believe that. But what is obvious is that too many lives have been lost in these butterfly nets. We need safer fishing," Antonio said.

"You mean Bradley Hart's plans? You're on board with them?"

Antonio gave a slow shrug. "I don't want to be, but what choice do we have? We can't have our sons - our fathers -

dying out there. Mr Hart's plans are ambitious but... well... he showed us a presentation of his company's records. Very profitable and very safe."

"It will be sad to see the butterfly fishing go, but not as sad as losing a son. I would tell anyone here to choose the new fishing and save their men's lives," Donna said with a nod. Her eyes shone with determination.

"These plans are letting you see that Miguel's death won't be in vain?" I asked.

"Exactly. That's exactly what Mr Hart said. Miguel's death will prevent others. That comforts us, doesn't it?" Antonio answered.

Donna nodded.

"Do you think we can trust him?" Jose asked.

"We have to, son. It can't carry on like this. And he's an impressive businessman. Even now on his vacation he has reams of paperwork and reports he can show us. We can't continue like this, with good men dying."

"Of course," Jose agreed.

Donna let out a shaky sigh from her position at the end of the table, and Antonio reached over and rubbed her arm. "Go and rest, we're about done here."

Donna bid us goodbye and retreated out of the room. Only when we had heard the soft click of the bedroom door closing behind her did Antonio talk. "My wife is finding it hard. Forgive her."

"There's no forgiveness needed. It must be a very difficult time for you both. We'll leave you," I said.

As we all filed out of the neat house, I took one look back at the formica table. Antonio's paper remained there, his expensive pen unused.

He had placed his trust in us and I hoped he wouldn't regret it.

10

———

Jose returned home to check on Maria, and Cornelius and I decided to wander the island a little.

We found a roadside cafe and took a table outside, where we could watch life pass us by.

"This isn't the holiday I expected for us, lassie," Cornelius said after a young waitress brought us glasses of tepid water and small cups of strong coffee.

The sun beat down on the street and I was glad that we were shielded under a fabric awning. The nights were frigid, but the days were hotter than anything I'd experienced before.

I thought I knew what a heatwave was, from the occasional English summers when I'd been able to wear t-shirts and shorts for a fortnight or more without needing to grab a jumper or a raincoat.

But the heat in Mexico was different. Every time I left the relative cool of the indoors, the heat surrounded me and swallowed me up. My skin was already looking darker, as if I'd had a lifetime of sun instead of the few days since I stepped off the airplane.

Cornelius looked every part the British traveller, with his open-toed sandals and socks pulled up towards his pale knees. His nose had burned and he'd started referring to himself as Rudolph.

"I hope we can get to the bottom of it all before we have to leave," I said as I watched a young boy race by, full of energy and excitement to get somewhere.

"I'm sure we will," Cornelius said with a wink.

"I can't believe my mum came to Mexico," I said.

Cornelius raised a ridiculous eyebrow.

"In my memory, she was so cautious. And she'd never have spent the money on something as indulgent as a holiday just for herself," I explained.

I thought back to the spartan houses we had lived in. Each move was quick and industrious as we followed my dad's work around the country with our few possessions. It was a point of pride for my mum that we could pack up and be gone within an hour or so, leaving no sign that we'd ever even been there.

And yet... there were the days when I had caught her. When I'd found her looking at old photographs of herself, or experimenting with make-up when she was usually plain faced. She'd pray for forgiveness after those occasions.

Her vanity was her weakness, or that's what she'd told me.

Dad had shrugged his shoulders during those times. He'd told her that enjoying a little fun wouldn't hurt her, but mum hadn't been convinced.

I seemed to understand that having a little fun already had hurt her, and she wasn't going to give it a second chance.

"I've noticed you stealing glances at Jose. You like him,

don't you, lassie?" Cornelius said as his red nose shone, even out of the sunlight.

"He's nice," I said with a shrug. I knew that my cheeks were flaming almost as much as his nose, but tried to act nonchalant.

"Holiday romances are a rite of passage for a young person," he ploughed ahead regardless of my obvious discomfort.

"I'm not interested in a holiday romance, Uncle C. But, are you talking from experience?" I asked, to change the subject.

He waggled his eyebrows at me. "What do you think?"

"I think a handsome young reindeer like you would have had his pick of the prettiest doe!"

Cornelius met my gaze for a second, realised what I'd just done, and then spluttered a mouthful of bitter coffee all over the small table between us. I hastily reached for a paper towel and wiped up the mess as he continued to laugh and cough.

"Well, lassie! Well, I see how you're playing it! A young reindeer like me! Very good! Although they're not called does. Reindeers share their gender names with cattle - the male is a bull, sometimes a stag admittedly, and the female is a cow. The babies are called calves. Don't say your Uncle Cornelius is nothing but a good time guy. I can teach you a thing or two as well!"

"I didn't doubt it for a second," I said. My uncle was full of facts, trivia and information. I didn't doubt its existence, or its vastness, although I did sometimes question its reliability.

We sat in a companionable silence for a few moments until I remembered what we'd been talking about before my reindeer gag.

"You didn't answer. Have you had a holiday romance? Or... wait... did my mum?" I asked. A shudder ran through me as I considered my mum, not just who she was before me. But who she was before my dad.

Cornelius met my gaze and smiled at me. "She did, lassie."

"But... she never said. I did ask her questions, you know. Not as many as I wish I had now. I thought I'd have a whole lifetime to get to know her. But, all she ever talked about was her and dad, as if her life had started with him."

"In a way, it did," Cornelius said. He took a long guzzle of the water.

I decided to do the same. It had grown warm and clammy, but it still refreshed the tastebuds after the bitterness of the coffee.

"Was dad her holiday romance?" I asked, confused.

"No, no. His chapter started soon after her holiday romance."

"Were you in touch with her then?" I asked.

"I was always in touch with *her*, lassie. She just chose not to return that contact for a good few years. And she had her reasons. But we got on well then, sure. As well as we could considering the age difference. And, I guess she'd have been closer to a sister than a brother."

"Did the rift start because you didn't like my dad?" I asked as the idea occurred to me.

He shook his head and his jowls wobbled. "I had no issue with your dad. And I don't believe your dad's ever had an issue with me. I know I can be cantankerous at times and there are people who find it hard to stomach old Cornelius, but I wasn't quite as set in my ways back then. Your dad's a good man, and that was all I had to care about him. Would he look after my sister and my niece? And he did that, nobody can deny it."

"So what happened? Please tell me."

"Not yet, lassie. It will all be revealed, I promise you that. But for now just pay attention to that fluttery feeling you get when Jose is around. Your mum experienced similar. You're following in her footsteps and experiencing some of what she did as a young woman," Cornelius said mysteriously.

"Fine. Keep your secrets. I still can't imagine my mum being in Mexico, though. I wish she'd talked to me about it," I murmured.

Cornelius shot me a resigned smile but said nothing, and I was swept away in my own thoughts. There was no way I could picture my mum - Isadora Monk - experiencing this heat or being so open to new people that a holiday romance would develop.

I sighed and finished my coffee.

Cornelius laughed. "Do you have to pull that face when you drink it, lassie? You'll scare the sun out of the sky!"

I grinned. "It's so much stronger than my coffee back home! I like it, it's just a bit of a shock each time I taste it."

"You'll get used to it. Are you finished?"

I nodded and we paid the bill and left. The streets were lively, as always, and as we walked, we passed a pair of older men playing guitar and singing in front of a brightly coloured wall mural.

As we reached a street of open-fronted shops, I had an idea, and grabbed a few pairs of underwear and a new t-shirt and pair of shorts.

Uncle Cornelius laughed at me. "You've ran out?"

"I didn't bring a change of knickers. Did you?" I admitted with a laugh.

Cornelius nodded his head as I paid. "I never leave

home without a change of clothes. Anything could happen, lassie. Best to be prepared!"

"Hmm," I grumbled. "Maybe you could have shared that piece of wisdom before we left the hotel?"

"Ah, yes, that could have been an idea actually. Oops!"

We continued exploring the island, wanting to give Jose and Maria some privacy but also feeling in no rush to leave the streets. I grinned as we walked past a playground, where children of all ages ran around and played.

We weaved through the town taking lefts and rights and going only where we thought looked interesting.

As we turned one corner, I spotted Luis from the hotel and waved to him.

He took a moment to place us and then grinned and came over.

"You came!"

"We certainly did, young man. We are intrepid travellers and we thrive on adventure, even if some of the bumpier parts of the bus journey played havoc with my piles," Cornelius happily explained.

"Anyway! We're so glad you told us about this place. It's incredible. I'll remember this trip for the rest of my life," I gushed.

Luis beamed at me. "I'm so pleased to hear that."

"Actually, Emily, I could do with a word with Luis. Give us a moment?"

I watched as Cornelius draped an arm around Luis and lead him to the narrow alley between two houses.

Cornelius spoke to him in hushed tones and then pulled out his wallet and placed a few notes in the man's hand. He glanced at his watch then, said a few more things that I couldn't hear, and then shook Luis' hand.

"What was that about?" I asked.

"Just had to see a man about a dog, lassie," Cornelius said with a wink.

"What does that mean?"

"Ah! Haven't you heard that before? It's just a little phrase I picked up somewhere. Popular in the midlands, I believe. Nothing for you to worry your head about, though."

We continued on our way and as our stomachs started to grumble, I saw Bradley Hart sitting alone outside a cafe and elbowed Cornelius to alert him.

"Ouch!" My uncle exclaimed, a tad more dramatically than I thought was really necessary.

"Shh! Look over there, it's Bradley Hart. Let's get some lunch at the table next to him and see if we can learn more about his plans," I suggested.

"Good idea, lassie. Lead the way!"

We entered the shade of the covered area and I made sure that I didn't look in Bradley's direction until we'd sat down. I'd planned to lean over and say hello when sat down, so it didn't look as if we'd sat there just to be near him, but before I'd taken my seat, Bradley spoke.

"Get the plans drawn up ASAP," he barked, and my head swung around to see who he was talking to. He was alone at the table and there was nobody else close to him apart from Cornelius and I. Surely he wasn't speaking to us?

I frowned at Cornelius, who began making complicated hand gestures towards his ears. I had no idea what he was trying to communicate.

"The clock's ticking here and we're on a tight deadline. I need to be in Kuala Lumpur next week and this project has to be finalised before I leave," Bradley continued.

I leaned in to Cornelius and whispered. "Who is he talking to?"

"He's on handsfree," Cornelius said.

"Handsfree?" I repeated. It was a phone thing, I knew that much. Okay. So, somehow the Texan was speaking on the phone without his phone being in his hands, never mind near his mouth.

Cornelius tapped his ear again and I turned and looked at Bradley. Finally, I spotted the tiny flash of white sitting in his ear.

The flash of white had no wire, was connected in no way to the mobile phone that sat on the table in front of him, and was smaller than my thumbnail, but it would appear that it was magically allowing him to have a phone conversation.

I gave a nonchalant nod as if that sight hadn't just blown my technophobic mind.

"Don't bring me problems, Bill, bring me solutions. Here's the thing. Get it to me in the next hour or your next project might just be uploading your own job description onto a few job sites. Now, are we on the same page?" Bradley barked into the phone.

I side-eyed him, but he wore sunglasses and the Stetson sat back atop his head, so I could make out little about his expression. His tone didn't sound like he was joking, but I was no expert on the American sense of humour.

A waitress approached and brought us a small bowl of olives.

We ordered more water, more coffee, and tamales.

After a minute of silence from the other table, I felt reasonably confident that Bradley had ended the call (how?!), and made a show of looking in his direction and pretending to notice him for the first time.

"Oh! Oh, hello there! You're the fishing guy, right? From America?" I exclaimed.

I noticed Cornelius raise an eyebrow. I'd probably over-done the excitement in my voice a little.

"Bradley Hart," the American said. He offered his hand and I shook it, then watched as he did the same to Cornelius.

"Good to see you," Cornelius said. His voice was a little more polished than normal and I wondered if perhaps I wasn't the only one feeling nervous about speaking to such a high-powered businessman.

"I guess I stand out here, the only person in a Stetson. You fine folks ever been to Texas?" Bradley asked. His demeanour with us compared to his tone on the phone call was a big shift and I wondered which was the real him, if any.

"No, sir," Cornelius said. I frowned at him. He never addressed anyone as sir. In fact, if one of his favourite stories was to be believed, he'd once met the Queen and greeted her as Lizzie.

"Well, I'm from Dallas, and believe it or not, this is common attire over there. Everyone you see walking the city has on a Stetson and a fine pair of cowboy boots. Doesn't matter if they're shopping or conducting their business. It's the way we dress. I guess I forget sometimes that other places don't do the same. Now, the thing with a Stetson is, once you've worn one, you'll never want to take it off. It keeps you cool, blocks the sun , protects your head from burning. I happen to think it looks mighty cool, too," Bradley said with a wink.

The waitress approached his table and placed a large salad and steak in front of him. He waited for her to leave and then turned his attention back to Cornelius and I.

"Great place, huh? Beautiful. You came to the town hall?"

"The town hall?" I asked.

"Sorry, doing it again. Town hall, it's what we Yanks say to describe a big meeting. You were there?"

"Oh, yes, we were there," I agreed. I was pleased he'd broached the subject first and wondered if he was going to talk about his plans with us freely.

"How did I do? You fine folks must have seen a few big talks before. Politicians and whatnot. Did I do okay?"

I shifted in my seat a little. Seriously? He wanted feedback? "Well, erm, I'm not sure that I'm the person to ask about that."

"Emily here hasn't seen that many talks. I have, though, and I have to say Mr Hart you were captivating. You held the crowd's attention and you spoke plainly. I was impressed," Cornelius said with a vigorous nod.

Bradley nodded but showed no sign of pleasure or surprise at the compliments. "I agree. I really had them listening, didn't I? It's not always easy as an outsider but I spent a lot of time preparing that talk and getting the tone right. In fact, you might have overheard me on a call just now?"

Cornelius and I said nothing, not wanting to commit either way.

"Well, that guy I was talking to, he's supposedly one of the rising stars in the company. I tell you he feels like a dead weight around my shoulders a lot of the time. I tell him what to do and he brings me objections. I tell him to find solutions, not problems. That's why I pay him, right? Anyway, he's going to get everything finalised today, so tomorrow will be the start of a whole new era for Janitzia Island."

"Really? That fast?" I exclaimed as I cringed at him getting the name of the island wrong again.

Bradley mistook my shock for excitement. "Impressive, ain't it? With these deals, we have to move fast. So many moving parts."

"And lives at risk," I said.

"And lives at risk! Give the girl a gold star! That's exactly right, bingo! Now, I tell you fine folks, this is a pretty good steak but you ever find yourself in Dallas, you look me up and I'll show you where to find a real steak."

I smiled at him. There was something strangely alluring about Bradley Hart, but I had the strong suspicion that if Cornelius and I turned up in Dallas next week, he would have no idea who we were and would probably refuse to see us.

Next week. I thought back to his phone call.

"You're on vacation, right? Are you heading on to anywhere after this?" I asked.

Bradley chewed, then took a sip of water. "I could be anywhere next week. The holiday will be over, put it that way! I'll go where I'm needed."

"Ah," I said. "We're staying in Mexico City."

Bradley nodded as he shoved another forkful of food into his mouth.

Our own food came and Bradley started to scroll on his phone. The conversation, it seemed, was over. I wondered how much Bradley Hart charged his time out at and what I'd have been billed for that brief conversation if it had been on the clock.

I was quickly distracted by the food, though. The tamales were delicious.

When we'd finished eating, Bradley was still at the table, but he had turned away from us slightly and propped his right arm on the table. His body language gave the impression that he didn't want to be interrupted, and so we paid and left without even a goodbye.

As we tried to weave our way back through the streets to Maria's home, I replayed the brief conversation with Bradley in my head.

"You were very respectful towards Bradley. Calling him sir and Mr Hart," I said.

"I've met an American businessman once or twice in my time, lassie. They hold us English up on a bit of pedestal."

"Do they?" I asked.

"Oh, yes. And that's fine with a lot of folks, but those high-powered sorts, it can become a bit of a peacock fight. Showing off your feathers and all that. Much better to just show respect and let them think they're the top dog."

I wasn't quite sure what all of the animals had to do with anything but I saw his point. Being shown such obvious respect had probably relaxed Bradley Hart enough to speak to us.

"And what did you think to him?"

"I think he knows exactly where he'll be next week, and I think he saw an opportunity for his own business and acted fast. You heard the pressure he was putting on that poor employee of his to get everything sorted ASAP!"

"A case of good timing for him, that he happened to be here?"

"You know what they say about luck, lassie? The harder a person works, the luckier they become."

"What does that mean?" I asked.

"Well, we heard good old Mr Hart say he's in Kuala Lumpur next week. You know what struck me about that? Their fish consumption is some of the highest in the world."

"No! Are you suggesting that he spends his time travelling to other places in the hopes that his business can get involved with their fishing?"

Cornelius shrugged his broad shoulders. "I'm just saying I'd be very surprised if this is his first time here. For all we know, he could have been visiting for years, getting the contacts in place, so that at the first opportunity his company was the obvious choice to hand the fishing over to."

"Do companies really operate like that?" I asked. I was absolutely stunned. Even more stunned than I had been by Bradley Hart's handsfree set up.

"Like that, and a lot worse," Cornelius said.

We turned a corner and saw Maria's pretty little house up ahead. I felt my stomach flip a little at the thought of seeing Jose again, and followed Cornelius' advice. I tried to imagine my mum, abroad and feeling similar anticipation for a young man who would woo her for a holiday romance.

The thought made me smile. The Isadora Monk I knew had lived a life of service, of abstinence and self-imposed rules. The idea of her being giddy with the first blossom of romance made me happy beyond belief.

Good for you, mum.

We knocked at the door and Jose himself answered. His eyes adjusted from the relative dark of inside to the bright sun of the outside world, and he beamed when he saw us.

"Where have you travellers been? Have you had fun?"

"We've had a lovely time. How's your mum doing?" I said.

Maria waved to us from the settee and I saw that Miss Lulu was curled up on her lap.

I laughed. "You're losing the battle about dogs in the house, I see."

Jose rolled his eyes. "I'm giving them a free pass for a few days. Given everything that's happened. Have you found anything new?"

"We had a chat with Bradley Hart. The plans for the transfer of the fishing should be all finished today," Cornelius shared.

Jose closed his eyes and muttered under his breath. "This is a sad day indeed."

"It has to happen, son. We can't lose any more lives," Maria said. She fussed the stray dog's ears absentmindedly as she spoke.

"I know, mama. But I think dad would be so sad to see this happen."

"Your father and Francisco. And many more. But we have to allow change to come," Maria insisted.

"Do you think people will treat you better in the future?" I asked.

Maria shook her head and pulled Miss Lulu close, buried her face in the dog's fur.

Jose opened his mouth to object, then stopped himself.

I realised that Maria was crying, her shoulders heaving as she clung to the dog.

"What is it?" I asked.

"Mama's agreed to move away with me. We're going to have a fresh start," Jose said. His voice was forlorn and it was clear that Maria was not pleased to have made the agreement.

"Well, congratulations! That's exciting news!" Cornelius boomed, either ignoring or not seeing the emotion in the room with us.

"You know, I had a fresh start recently myself," I said.

Maria peeked out at me from Miss Lulu's fur. "You did?"

I nodded. "I'd always lived a very sheltered life, taken no chances. I decided to take a chance and I visited Cornelius.

We'd been out of touch for many years, but he welcomed me into his home and his life, and he suggested we have this adventure. I'd never even been on a plane before!"

"Really? That's very brave of you, Emily. Well done," Jose said. There was a glint of something in his eyes - admiration, perhaps. I looked away.

"That's wonderful. It really is. I've moved away before, remember? I know that I can do that. But I'd be leaving Daniel behind."

I shook my head, surprised by how strongly I objected to her words. "No. You wouldn't. You couldn't. I lost my mum. When I left my old home, I left her behind too, following your logic. But it doesn't work that way. She's everywhere. I feel her with me every day. Daniel will always be with you, Maria. You carry him in your heart."

11

———

In the mid-afternoon, Maria retreated to her bedroom to begin packing. Miss Lulu accompanied her and every so often the soft tones of Maria talking to the dog carried out into the living room.

"Are you taking the dog with you?" I asked with a cheeky grin.

Jose laughed. "I think so. Honestly, if it makes her happier about leaving, I don't care. I'll even get the animal a tag and microchip her. I just want to see mama live her life again and stop hiding away."

"I think she'll be okay."

"We can hope. What you said about your mum earlier, it was really beautiful. I think losing a parent makes us grow up faster."

"Really? Yeah... maybe," I said. I didn't know whether I agreed with that. I still felt very young and very inexperienced in the world, but I was growing in confidence every day.

"We've reached a dead end with the investigation?" Jose

asked. I could see that he was trying to keep his tone light but that he desperately wanted an update. He wanted to know the truth about his dad's death. Of course he did.

"No, not at all. I was actually wondering if you'd take me and show me your dad's boat," I said.

He flinched a little.

"Or I can go alone, if you can just tell me where to head," I offered.

"No, no. It might be good for me to see the thing again," he said.

"Are you coming, Uncle C?" I asked.

Cornelius had collapsed into a chair and was watching TV. "I'm afraid this darn chair hasn't finished with me yet, lassie. But I just heard that there's another meeting tonight. It's at seven. Shall I meet you there?"

"Sounds good," I agreed. My heart sank. Another meeting.

Jose and I set off through the streets, weaving in between tourists and locals alike, and ignoring the calls from the food sellers to try their ware.

We reached the waterfront and stopped for a few moments to gaze out.

The water was so still and looked so clear, it was hard to believe that it was responsible for so much tragedy.

Boat after boat was lined up, most empty but some the hub of activity. I saw a sleeping fisherman on at least two of the boats, and a third had a pair of men gutting fish, the work making their hands and t-shirts dirty.

"It's hard to believe that all of this will be gone," Jose said.

"These men will still fish, though. They'll still be out on the water, just in a safer way," I said.

"We'll see. But even if they are, they'll be working for the man, clocking in and out, with no control over their time any more. A fisherman here is his own boss. Literally the master of his own ship. It will be a big change."

I nodded. I could see how difficult that change would be. And yet... if it meant that lives would be saved, surely it was worth making those changes?

"Come on," Jose said. I walked next to him, the sun beating down on my skin. Stray dogs ran around our feet, almost tripping us up.

"You're trying with the wrong Lopez! I won't be taking you home," Jose spoke to the animals with a laugh.

We reached the very end of the row of boats and Jose indicated to the last one. It was tiny, big enough for two men who really liked each other, but it was brightly coloured and seemed in good condition. If there had been any damage caused the night of Daniel's death, it had been fixed since.

"This is it. My dad's favourite place in the world," Jose said. He gazed at the boat and seemed to zone out, transported away to memories of his father.

"It's beautiful," I said. "How does it work? He sits there and casts the net?"

Jose shook his head. "No, he stood up a lot of the time. They all stand up a lot. The net is really huge. You haven't seen one?"

I shook my head.

Jose looked out across the water and spotted a boat not far from the shore. He pointed to it. "There, see the net?"

I looked and saw that the man in that boat was standing up and holding a circular net that spanned almost the length of the boat. The end of the handle was in the water to his left, and the rim of the net itself was elevated higher than the man's head on his right. The bottom of the net was submerged in the water, catching fish as the boat glided through the water.

"Wow. That's incredible," I said.

"Yeah, it's really something," Jose agreed.

"What are they catching?"

"Mainly *pescado blanco*. Whitefish. It's the island speciality, I guess."

"I've tried it. It's really good," I said. I felt the need to pinch myself. Was I really standing on a Mexican island talking about the local delicacy?

I knelt down and took a closer look at the boat. Two people had died in the same way on it, and yet it gave no clues.

"What are you looking for?" Jose asked.

"I don't know," I admitted. "Clues. I can't see any damage. Does it look how you remembered it?"

Jose looked at the boat and nodded. "It's the same."

"So it hasn't been repaired at all? You said you weren't sure if there could have been any damage," I pressed.

"No, not that I can see. I guess it's possible that someone could have fixed it up after dad's death without telling us, just to help us out. But not that likely. Word spreads on a small island. We would have heard about it. And nothing's changed since Miguel's death. There hasn't been enough time. Fixing a boat that isn't being used wouldn't be anyone's priority."

"So we have an undamaged boat. I guess the nets themselves wouldn't give us any clues?"

"They burned the net that dad was found in. Nobody liked the idea that someone else could have used that net. It seemed like bad luck. So it was burned."

"Okay. That makes sense," I said. From a common sense

point of view, it really did. Although as evidence storing, it was probably not the best process to follow.

I watched as Jose took a step and climbed aboard the boat. He sat down and gazed out at the water, lost in his thoughts.

My thoughts were that the boat was so small, it must be easy to lose balance and find yourself out in the water, tangled in the web. Easy, and devastating.

"I've seen everything I need to. I'll leave you on your own for a bit," I said.

Jose turned and gave me a grateful smile, a nod of his head. I walked away, then turned back after a few steps, and looked at the silhouette of him, looking completely at peace as he sat in the same spot his father had loved so much.

As I continued along my way, I decided to stop at a small waterfront cafe and enjoy a cold drink. The can of fizzy orange was brought to me by an older man who seemed to size me up with interest.

"You're the one who went to see the Sanchez family," he said after a few seconds.

It took me a moment to realise who he was speaking about. Antonio and Donna.

"Yes, I went to pay my respects," I said with a smile.

"That boy was always going to end up in trouble one way or another. Chasing his dreams instead of living his life. I did warn him, you know."

"Warn him?" I asked.

"He wasn't a good enough fisherman to be out there on his own and I said that to him. Of course, the young don't listen."

"Wait," I said. "You saw Miguel take the boat out?"

"No, I'd closed up by then."

"I don't understand. What did you see exactly?" I asked.

"I didn't see anything. I heard Miguel being offered the job. Sounded too good to be true to me, and I'm old enough to know that anything that sounds too good to be true normally is."

"What job was it?"

The proprietor sighed, apparently sick of me not understanding. "A fishing job, obviously. A man needed someone to do a night's fishing but he didn't have a boat. He asked if Miguel had one, and that boy's eyes lit up. Of course, he had no boat but we all know that Daniel Lopez's boat is still out there."

"He was offered money?"

"Too much money. Way too much. It set alarm bells off to me. The other fellow left and Miguel had this stash of money, an envelope full of it. He was the big man then, in his head! Ordering beers for everyone. I told him to put his money away and think about what he was doing."

"But he wouldn't listen?"

"*Calm down, old man,* that's what he said. He told me it was one night's work with more coming. Francisco had let him go, and not without his reasons, so I guess Miguel was needing some cash. I told him at least go and take that money home and speak to your parents, but who knows whether he listened."

"He didn't," I said. "His parents had no idea why he was on the boat."

The man chewed his lip and nodded. "I expected as much."

"Who was the man offering the work?" I asked.

He shrugged. "I don't know."

"Did you see him? Can you describe him?"

"It's the busiest time of year in here. I was rushed off my feet and of course Luisa had to get home early so it was just me. I only heard what I heard because they were sat next to the bar, but I could hear them not see them."

I tried to hide my disappointment.

The man began to cackle. "Here's a description for you. Man in a sombrero! That's who you're looking for. Good luck finding one of them in Mexico!"

I smiled at the man and finished my drink, then walked the short distance to the Sanchez home.

I knocked on the door and Donna answered.

"Oh, Emily? Hello again. Antonio's at work," she said as she held the door open.

"Can I come in?" I asked.

She nodded and closed the door behind me. "Have you heard anything?"

"I think so. If Miguel had something valuable to keep safe, where would he put it?" I asked.

Donna furrowed her brows. "Valuable? In his bedroom, maybe. You're welcome to look."

She showed me the way to his room and I smiled as I entered. It was the bedroom of a teenager, not a young man. The walls were covered with posters of celebrities and football players, and the one poster he had of a woman was a very respectful and fully-dressed dark haired beauty who I didn't recognise.

He had a bookcase full of old school books, picture books that must have been his favourite as a child, and football trophies. On his bedside table was a lamp shaped like a football, and a glass of water that I guessed had been left since he last touched it.

I pulled open the top drawer by his bedside and saw the envelope on top of a pile of well-organised toiletries.

I opened the envelope and saw the notes, brand new and full of deadly potential.

From the doorway, Donna gasped. "Where did he get that?"

"Miguel was paid by someone to go out on the boat. Do you know anyone who would ask him to do that?"

Donna shook her head, her eyes wide and her hand covering her mouth. "Nobody! Who would ask a boy who can't fish to go out alone? It makes no sense. He must have been paid for something else. Not fishing."

"He was paid to fish. I've spoken to someone who overheard the conversation and tried to warn Miguel not to do it."

"Oh no," Donna crumpled to the floor and began to cry.

"I don't know who gave him this money. Does he have wealthy friends? Anyone who might ask him to do them a favour?"

Donna shook her head. "There are so many fishermen here, why on earth ask Miguel to do it? Why not ask someone who does it every day, who has a boat? It makes no sense."

"I agree," I said. As a plan, asking Miguel to fish made about as much sense as asking a fish to climb a tree. He didn't have the skill or the experience. If he hadn't been so young and gung-ho, he would have known that accepting the work was a dangerous decision.

I wondered about the person who had paid cash for their fish and never had it arrive. Why hadn't that person revealed themselves and asked for their money to be returned? Did they realise that they had sent an immature boy to their death? Were they devastated with grief?

And then another thought occurred to me. Maybe they had never expected Miguel to return to the land. Maybe they had known that the fishing trip would be deadly. Maybe the cold hard cash in that envelope next to his Lynx deodorants and other boyhood trappings was blood money. A price worth paying to have another fisherman dead.

But who would do that? Who would want that, and why?

"You know what happened, don't you?" Donna said.

"Not yet. But I think I'm getting closer. I think I'm going to have it all worked out soon for you," I promised.

12

———

The comfortable chair still hadn't finished with Cornelius when I returned to the Lopez home. In fact, he was fast asleep with his mouth hanging open.

I padded past him and down the narrow hallway, where I heard Maria and Jose chatting in her bedroom.

They looked up and flashed me a smile as I approached.

"I'm sorry. Have his snores forced you in here?" I asked, just as another enormous snore reverberated through the house.

Maria laughed and shook her head. "We were reminiscing about Daniel. Jose told me that this trip has something to do with your mum, Emily?"

I nodded. "She came to Mexico on holiday when she was eighteen."

"Ah, so you're doing what she did?"

"I'm not sure. I think there's something more to it, but I don't know what. I think something happened to her when she was here," I said. I'd been desperately trying to work out the reason for the trip, but I couldn't figure it out.

"It must have been a big trip for her as a young person. I'm sure it changed her in many ways. This trip will change you too," Maria said. She looked at me with a fondness that was almost maternal and I swallowed the emotion away.

"It's already changed me. I'm seeing things and meeting people and I'm so much more confident than I was," I agreed.

Maria reached over and squeezed my hand. "Your mama must be so proud of you."

My eyes watered and I bit my lip. All I could do was nod. I hoped she was proud. I knew that I was proud of her.

Cornelius' words came to me: remember being proud of her.

The weight of those words hit me afresh and I realised. Something had happened. There was something in my mum's life that might change my opinion of her. Something linked to this place, to Mexico.

"I'm proud of her. I'll always be proud of her," I said. My voice shook. Saying the words out loud felt like making a vow.

I didn't care what Cornelius revealed about my mum. I would always love her and remember her with pride. Or at least, I hoped I would.

The snoring had stopped and in the silence I heard shuffling around in the living room. I turned and saw Cornelius standing by the front door.

"It was a mighty battle, but I have prevailed," he declared with a look across to the chair he had just escaped from.

"Congratulations. Where are you off to?"

"Time is of the essence, Emily. We'll be clearing Maria's name before she moves on to her next chapter. I'm guessing you've worked out our next move?"

I considered his question, and the new information I'd gathered while he was having a siesta. "Actually, I have. Let's go."

We promised to meet Maria and Jose for the evening meeting, and set off through the busy streets. We passed a procession of musicians, all playing upbeat music and wearing traditional clothes as they weaved through the streets.

"So, did you enjoy your nap?" I couldn't resist teasing him.

"Jet lag is an awful thing, lassie. My mind was alert, I can assure you of that. I had the most captivating dreams. There was one that involved an old love interest. Goodness me, I haven't thought of Barbara in forty years or more! Now, she was a woman who knew what she wanted."

I eyed him. "What happened to her?"

"Well, erm, it turned out she didn't want me!"

"Oh," I said, flustered by the awkward end to the story.

"She went off to bigger and better things. Backpacking around Australia! She invited me, but I had to say no. I had the house to renovate, of course. So off she went with promises of how we'd meet again in the future if it was meant to be. I think she married a surfer over there. Anyway, that's enough of that. I'm guessing you didn't just sit around and wait for me to wake up, so what have I missed?"

I brought Cornelius up to date and felt delighted by how interested he was. He gasped and exclaimed at all of the right points.

"Poor Miguel. I can remember how it was to be a young dreamer. He was really taken advantage of," Cornelius said with a shake of his head.

"I think so," I agreed.

We reached the government buildings and I pushed open the heavy door and made my way towards the reception desk.

"I'm here to see Antonio Sanchez," I told the man who sat behind the desk.

The man frowned. "I believe he's in a meeting. I can check. Can I take your name?"

"I'm Emily Monk, and this is my Uncle Cornelius," I explained.

The man picked up the phone on his desk and dialled a five digit extension number. After a minute, he hung up.

"He isn't answering. If you'd like to take a seat, you can wait for him," the man offered.

"Sure, we'll do that," I agreed.

The seats were very plush and I heard myself let out an involuntary groan as I sank into one. I eyed Cornelius and leaned across to him.

"I hope this chair doesn't have the same effect as the last one you sat in," I said with a wink.

He roared with laughter and attracted the gaze of the office workers who milled around the reception in smart dress.

A few minutes passed and then I watched as Bradley Hart, in his trademark Stetson, sauntered across the lobby with a smile on his face.

"You have a great day!" He called out to the receptionist, who beamed at him and returned the sentiment.

"Well, look who it is," Uncle C said. He probably meant it to be said under his breath, but he seemed incapable of using a quiet voice, and Bradley looked across at us.

Before I knew it, I'd waved at him. Actually waved, as if I was across the street from him and not just a couple of feet away.

"Hello, Mr Hart. Fancy seeing you here," I said with a smile as he approached us.

"You gotta call me Bradley! You call me Mr Hart and I'm thinking I'm in trouble! What brings you fine folks down here? It's an awful nice day, you should be out sightseeing," he gushed.

"We're here to see someone. And I could say the same for you, you're on holiday too. Why aren't you out there relaxing?"

He shrugged his wide shoulders. "Turns out that this whole fishing situation's more urgent than my days in the sun. I was just in a meeting now and there's a lot of factors, all important factors, and let's just say that things need to get a move on."

"It's been decided, then? For definite?" I asked.

"Oh, sure, sure. And I'm just one cog in a big system, you fine folks will understand that. I happened to be here and have a plan I could suggest. Thankfully it's all going to work out and we can save some lives. That's better than any holiday, don't you think?"

"Absolutely! It's an incredible turn of fate that you were here when needed, Mr Hart. Did you say you'd been here before?" Cornelius asked.

Bradley's perfectly white teeth were on show as his smile fixed in place, but he glanced down at his watch. "Gosh, I better dash. I have a call that I just can't be late for. Now you fine folks have a great day and I'll no doubt see you at the meeting tonight!"

"You certainly will," Cornelius and I both said at the same time.

And Bradley Hart was on his way, his mobile phone pressed to his ear before the door had closed behind him.

No sooner had he gone than we heard footsteps

approach us on the tiled floor. I looked up and saw Antonio, dressed in a full suit and tie, his black shoes polished to within an inch of their lives.

"Emily. Cornelius. Is everything okay?" His eyes darted between us.

"Oh, yes. Sorry, I didn't mean to trouble you. Is there somewhere we can talk?"

Antonio lead us to his office on the second floor. It was a lovely space, complete with a hardwood desk and leather chairs. He took a seat behind the desk and gestured for us to sit on the other side.

"Coffee?" He offered.

We declined. "We won't take up much of your time. We just saw Bradley Hart leaving."

Antonio nodded. "I was in a meeting with him. Not just me, there were around twenty of us."

"The meeting was about the fishing changes?"

"Yes. His lawyers have sent over quite the contract and it needs to be signed today, which is an issue because our counsel is on vacation."

"Surely you can have more time. What's the urgency?" Cornelius vocalised my thoughts.

Antonio shrugged. "Something about Mr Hart only making deals of this size in person. Apparently his diary is booked solid for six months, so we sign now or we lose the opportunity."

"That doesn't sound fair," I said.

"Unfortunately, we need him more than he needs us. Anyway, it's being signed. He gave us a couple of hours to confer but he suggested we sign it at tonight's meeting so the whole island can see and celebrate."

"That's a nice idea, but isn't there alternate counsel you can run the contract by before then? I knew a good lawyer a while back. Now what was his name? Barry, I think. Barry Donovan. Or was it Donovan Barrie? Great guy he was, though. He helped me challenge a parking ticket!" Cornelius asked.

I side-eyed Cornelius. I knew less than zero about the law but even I imagined that a specialist contract lawyer wouldn't sideline in parking tickets.

"I'll make a couple of calls, but this contract is over 500 pages long. Every clause has several sub-clauses. The language is very dry, it's not simple to read. Bradley Hart assures us that it's all standard terms and I have no reason to doubt him. He didn't come here to pitch us. We have a problem and he can solve it," Antonio said with a frown that made his moustache cover his lips completely.

"You think you should just trust him?" I asked.

"I think we have little choice. It would be reckless to turn away an offer of help after this series of deaths. I don't want that decision on my conscience."

"Of course. Nobody would. I just wonder if that makes the negotiating a little unbalanced," I said.

"This isn't a negotiation. Mr Hart has an offer and we can accept it or refuse it. He won't be negotiating."

Cornelius pulled his phone out of his pocket and tapped away at his screen.

Antonio watched him. "Look, I don't want to be rude but if there's nothing else, I have a lot to prepare before the meeting."

"Of course!" I exclaimed.

We assured Antonio that we could find our own way out, and left his office.

As soon as we were in the elevator, I asked, "What was that? Going on your phone while he was talking to us?"

Cornelius chuckled. "Sorry, lassie. I had an idea and I

didn't want to forget it! I find the old memory isn't what it used to be. I can tell you what I was wearing on August 16th, 1957, but other things just disappear out of my noggin!"

"I'm not sure it's age. It happens to me too. What was it you thought of?"

Cornelius looked at me blankly. "Oh! In there? The idea I had? Look at this."

He pulled his phone out and flicked across to his photo album, where he had screenshot a news article. He passed the phone to me and I read the article.

Bradley Hart comes to the aid of local residents following a spate of fishing accident deaths.

"What does this mean?" I asked.

"It's a couple of years old, but it reads as if this isn't the first time he's stepped in and offered his company as the solution to fishing deaths in another country," Cornelius explained.

"No wonder he was so quick to offer help now if he's done it before," I said.

"It makes sense. His company seems to go from success to success. He could be just what Janitzio Island needs."

"Hmm. Do you believe that, Uncle C?" I asked. There was still something unsettling to me about the idea of a rich foreign businessman sweeping in and saving the island.

Cornelius looked down at me and I saw the hesitation in his eyes.

"Wait here! I'll be right back," I called, as I sprinted back to the elevator. I pressed the button but I was too impatient to wait, and made a dash for the staircase. I sprinted up the first flight of stairs, then had to stop for a second to get my breath. The second flight of stairs I took at a much more sedate pace and silently vowed to start getting some regular exercise.

I barged into Antonio's office and found him bent over at his desk, studying a thick ream of papers that I guessed comprised the Hart Commercial contract. He looked up at the noise of me racing in, still panting, and looked at me curiously over the top of his glasses.

"Emily, what's happened?" He asked as he rose to his feet.

I shook my head as I got my breath back. "Don't... sign... anything."

UNCLE C'S WORLD WIDE WEB LOG

Rumours of Uncle C napping on the job are utterly false and not to be trusted.

Just saying, in case E (or not E) ever begins a rival web log. If that does happen, she may offer a certain youth and hip perspective, but I offer the truth!

Unrelated: discovered the most comfortable chair today. Very nice indeed. Highly recommend said chair for sitting in and STAYING AWAKE!

Onwards - the adventure continues!

Uncle C

13

I made sure we were nice and early for the evening meeting, but there was still quite the crowd of people when I filed in with Cornelius.

There was no sign of Jose and Maria yet, but they'd promised me they would attend. Even with their new life about to start, they wouldn't miss such an important announcement for Janitzio Island.

Cornelius and I took seats and I looked down to see that my hands were shaking.

"You okay, lassie?" Cornelius asked. He grabbed my tiny hands and covered them both with one of his own bear paws of flesh.

"I am," I said, and I pasted a determined smile on my face.

More and more people arrived, some eating tamales, others looking so nervous they could barely crack a smile. Antonio and Donna sat near the erected podium, along with the rest of the government workers. Donna met my gaze and smiled, then elbowed Antonio, who looked over at me and gave a nod.

My stomach fluttered.

Bradley Hart stomped across towards the government staff at one point, spoke with one high-ranking official, gesticulated a lot with his hands, and then marched away.

"Now's the time," Cornelius said.

I turned and looked behind us, searched the faces of the latecomers for Jose and Maria.

"They'll be here," Uncle C soothed.

I nodded and planted a kiss on my uncle's cheek, then rose to my feet. Doing that attracted no attention - plenty of people were standing rather than sitting, and lots of people were milling around and catching up with friends.

It wasn't until I left the audience and reached the theatre itself that a few people seemed to notice. Within the government staff in particular, people sat up straighter and watched my every move. My heart hammered in my chest as I approached the podium.

In what felt like slow motion, I stood behind the podium and looked out at the crowd. For a small island, it was incredible how many people lived there and had turned out for the meeting. I had been a girl who hated making presentations or reading aloud in class at school. I needed to find one friendly face to focus on or I'd certainly hyperventilate and lose my nerve.

I found Cornelius and smiled as he shot me an enthusiastic thumbs up.

My eyes continued to scan the crowd, past Josefina and several familiar faces of people whose names I didn't know or hadn't remembered, and eventually found Maria and Jose. My stomach fluttered at the confusion on their faces.

"Hello everyone. Good evening. My name's Emily and I wanted to talk to you before Mr Hart begins his own presentation," I said. My voice sounded tiny in the large space, even with the microphone, but to my surprise people settled down and listened to me. The people who had been standing found seats and the noise hushed.

"I arrived here for your Day of the Dead ceremony with my Uncle Cornelius, and we have been welcomed by your community. I didn't have the chance to meet Daniel Lopez, Francisco Martinez or Miguel Sanchez, but I have spent time with all of their families and I know they were all good men."

A round of sombre applause rang out from the audience.

"I know what it is to lose someone. My own mother died several years ago," I said. My eyes filled as I spoke of her. "In fact, we came to Mexico to follow in her footsteps and recreate a holiday she had when she was 18. I can't think of a better place for her to have travelled, or a nicer community for her to have met, than the people I have met since I arrived in your country."

More applause and a few whoops from the younger people in the audience rang out.

"Thank you. I'm very nervous about speaking to you tonight, but I have to. When my uncle and I arrived here, we were taken in by Maria Lopez and her son, Jose. I've heard and seen the way that Maria is treated because of the belief that she used witchcraft to kill her husband, and then Francisco and Miguel. I'm talking to you tonight to prove her innocence."

"You don't understand!" Someone called out from the audience.

I saw another couple of people shake their heads, get out of their seats and leave. I had to carry on before I lost my nerve completely.

"Please, listen to me. You're a community with three recent fishing deaths, and the terror that that causes you all to feel is the reason you're considering changing the way you fish."

I caught movement at the side of the space and saw Bradley Hart, arms folded, Stetson cocked back on his head. He glared at me as he realised that I wasn't some warm-up act singing his praises.

"Mr Hart here has a very successful fishing business. I can't deny that. And maybe the future with this deal is one where Janitzio Island becomes wealthier. Maybe the fishing becomes safer. But I have another scenario to share."

Bradley leaned in to the same high-ranking government official and whispered something to them. The official looked startled but met Bradley's gaze and shook his head.

At that point, Bradley Hart stalked across towards me.

"Ah, it's Mr Hart himself, let's give him a round of applause!" I thought on my feet and distracted him with the polite applause from the audience.

"As I was saying, there are a few different scenarios and I'd like to share them with you. The first is that Maria Lopez used witchcraft. But there's no evidence for that. It seems like a rumour that got out of hand quickly. Perhaps it was easier for this community to believe that than believe that a skilled fisherman like Daniel Lopez died in a tragic accident."

"Little girl, this is hardly relevant. I have a meeting scheduled and I'd like to get on with it," Bradley barked out. He was so good at projecting his voice that he didn't need the microphone.

"It's actually very relevant. And I won't be long," I assured him. "Maria Lopez adored her husband. He was a good husband and a good father. She liked Francisco and Miguel. Even if she was capable of causing their deaths, she had no reason to want any of them to die."

"She was punishing me!" Josefina called out from the audience.

"She wasn't," I insisted.

"So what's your explanation?" Josefina asked. Several people seated around her cheered to show her their support.

"Well, I'll admit that at first I thought it was a series of accidents. I supported Bradley Hart's changes because it seemed as though the fishing was too dangerous. But as I spoke to more people here, I learned that Daniel's death was the first fishing death in many years."

"That's true," Jose shouted.

"So, isn't it strange that there were no deaths for years and years, and suddenly there were three close together?"

"That's because it's witchcraft!" Josefina said.

"Josefina, I agree with you that all three deaths weren't natural. But it wasn't witchcraft either. Let's take a closer look at each of the deaths. Daniel Lopez was a skilled fisherman. He went out to fish while his wife was ill. He may have been distracted out there."

"Fishermen don't let land life distract them," someone in the front row of the audience said, with a knowing shake of his head.

"I'm sure they try not to, but they are only human. Francisco Martinez, another skilled fisherman. And then Miguel Sanchez, a younger man with no experience of fishing alone. I couldn't understand why he was even out on the water," I admitted.

"Neither could we," Antonio murmured from the side of the theatre.

"But I found out. I found out that Miguel had been paid to go out and fish. He'd been paid too much money. And isn't it strange that whoever paid him hasn't made a fuss about not getting the catch they paid for?"

"This is all fascinating, but let's get the meeting done with and then you can tell your little story," Bradley shouted. He made a move towards the podium and I shrank back, intimidated by the size of him.

Before he reached me, he was pushed back by a giant hand and I looked across and saw Uncle Cornelius stand between us. I'd never felt so grateful to see anyone in my life.

"You'll be letting the lassie finish, alright?" Cornelius said.

The crowd hollered at that, no doubt happy to see the American brought down to size a little.

"Now, I believe you were telling us about Miguel being paid to fish?" Cornelius prompted.

My cheeks flushed, I moved back closer to the microphone and took a breath. My voice still shook with nerves but I had to finish. "I started to think things over and I thought that maybe that money had never been for the fish, but to entice Miguel out onto the water so that he could be killed."

"She thinks she's Agatha Christie!" Bradley Hart exclaimed with a laugh. Nobody in the audience joined him.

"But who could want these fishermen to die? And then I realised the clues were all laid out for me. Miguel had been paid with a fat envelope full of new bank notes. What does that suggest? That he was paid by a tourist. Someone who had got their money at a currency exchange shop."

"Lots of tourists here at the moment, lassie," Cornelius said. Like Bradley, his voice was so booming that he had no need of the microphone to make himself heard.

"That's right. This would have to be a wealthy tourist,

though. It was a lot of money. I also know that the person who met with Miguel and offered him this work was wearing a sombrero. At least that's the way it was described. But as I thought about it all, I realised that a sombrero could look an awful lot like a Stetson in the dark."

Bradley's head snapped to attention. "What in the world are you suggesting? I'll have you know that I have thirteen different lawyers on speed dial. Just be careful before you say a word more, or these fine folks in the audience are all going to become witnesses in some serious litigation."

"I don't doubt you have all of those lawyers. In fact, I think you have eyes everywhere. That's how you were able to sweep in and help Fernatta Island three years ago, right?"

"Fernatta Island? What does that have to do with anything?" Bradley Hart asked.

"Three years ago Hart Commercial took over their fishing after a series of fishing deaths. That's worked quite well for you, hasn't it?"

He smirked. "I'd say it's worked better for them, ma'am. They're not dying anymore."

Several people in the audience gasped at the bluntness of his words.

"Well, there have been some deaths actually. Because part of the Fernatta Island contract is that those fishermen are required to work wherever needed. Your company's been sending them to much colder climates on big, commercial boats, and they're not used to those temperatures."

Bradley shrugged. "People die of illness or natural causes all the time. What's not happening anymore is fishing accidents that modern practices can put a stop to. Those people are very grateful."

"Really? They were trying to get out of the contract they signed before the ink had dried," I said. I didn't know that to be true, but Uncle Cornelius and I had spent a couple of hours looking at online message boards relating to Fernatta Island, and all did not seem to be running smoothly.

"This is completely irrelevant," Bradley said.

"Sorry, I'll get to my point. Despite the regrets that the people of Fernatta Island have about your deal, you've done very well out of it. You've gained a whole new workforce of cheap labour and taken control of their waters. They now can't fish their own waters."

"Because the way they were doing it was dangerous," Bradley said with exasperation.

"This is all news to me. Is this the same type of contract you're asking us to sign?" Antonio stood to his feet and asked.

"I'm not discussing the terms of the contract here. It's all signed and done," Bradley said.

"No, it isn't signed. We planned to sign now in front of the whole island," Antonio reminded him.

"Yes, of course. Well we can get the signing done and then speak about it at length. Let's not keep these fine folks waiting any longer than they need to. I'm sure they're not interested in this nonsense."

"Oh, we're very interested," Jose said. He rose from his seat and stood, hands on hips.

"Fine! You want me to admit that I profit from these deals? I'm a businessman, of course I do!"

"The Fernatta Island deal has worked very well for you, hasn't it?"

"Yes! Of course it has. I'm not a charity!" Bradley exclaimed.

"Some might say it's worked so well that you'd like to repeat it," I suggested.

"And here we are, repeating it. It's a win win solution for us all."

"Except it would be an extraordinary coincidence for both of these places to have spates of fishing deaths, wouldn't it?" I asked.

"Not really," Bradley said. "If the system is unsafe, people are going to die."

"But people weren't dying here, Mr Hart. There were no deaths before Daniel Lopez."

"And then two more very quickly. I'd say that's people dying. How many would need to die before you'd try to improve the system?"

"That depends on how many died in accidents and how many you killed," I said. I kept my tone even and held his gaze.

He glared at me and then turned and tried to make a run for it, but the government staff had predicted as much and surrounded him. Antonio grabbed one of his hands and other government staff held his other arm until they had him tight.

"Going somewhere?" I asked.

Bradley grunted. "I just, ah, forgot my glasses..."

"You won't be needing them. You can just listen to me. You killed Francisco Martinez and Miguel Sanchez. You killed them so that you could present yourself as the white knight coming to the island's rescue."

"Nonsense!" Bradley panted.

"You're very proud of your roots, Mr Hart. You've made sure it's well known that you can still get out there and handle a boat. You don't want people to imagine you're some back-office paper-pusher type of leader. You went out and grappled with Francisco, got him tangled in his net and then threw him over and left him to die."

"I didn't even know the man!"

"You didn't need to. All you needed was more fishermen to die, it didn't matter who they were," Cornelius said.

"But you actually chose a very skilled fishermen, and his death so soon after Daniel Lopez's spooked a lot of the other fishermen. So you had to trick someone into going out on the water. Miguel Sanchez was an easy target, a young man dreaming of a big break."

"You offered him that wad of cash and he really believed you were offering him a lucky break. The poor kid," Cornelius said with a shake of his head and a wobble of his jowls.

"This is ridiculous. You can't prove it," Bradley said.

Antonio looked up at the bigger man, his expression hard. "Miguel Sanchez was my son. You came into my office and offered me a deal to save lives, when you were the one taking them. How could you?"

"You don't believe this? Come on, you fine folks are smarter than this," Bradley said.

Antonio looked at me.

"I promised you I'd search for the truth, and this is it," I said.

He swallowed, the Adam's apple in his throat bobbing as he did. "We'll take him to the jail cell."

"Wait!" Maria's voice came from the audience. She looked at me desperately. "What about Daniel?"

I took another breath. "His death really was an accident. He wasn't killed, Maria. Bradley Hart wasn't here then. Daniel really did die in a tragic accident."

She began to cry and Jose scooped her into his arms. I watched as the people sitting close to her reached around and stroked her hair, held her hand, and murmured comfort to her. It was lovely to see, but I suspected it would still be too little, too late.

"Mr Hart, one last thing. We have CCTV showing you going out on the water after Francisco and Miguel, and we have the nets they were found in, which will be tested for your DNA. The evidence will prove that you killed those men. Why not give this community one bit of decency and tell them the truth?"

Bradley considered my words. He had that instinct for self-preservation, of course. But he also had a massive ego. The ego that had allowed him to build such an enormous company and make sure he took credit for all of its good decisions.

"You people wouldn't understand, but sometimes you have to suffer a little for the greater good. My company could have offered you a bright, bright future. We'd have fished these waters until there was only seaweed left! It would have been beautiful."

"But people had to die for you to do that?" Cornelius asked with his crazed eyebrows raised up on his lined forehead.

"Oh, heck no. I could have made that happen anytime. Those people had to die before you people saw the opportunity. So it's on all of your consciences, really. I just had to take drastic action to get y'all to see sense. A couple of lives in the grand scheme of things? It was a price worth paying. But not everyone has that business acumen like I do," he said.

I shook my head. "Take him away."

14

────────

Most of the crowd remained at the open air theatre after a group of government staff carted Bradley Hard away to the jail.

I was approached by many people who wanted to say thank you for my sleuthing work. I accepted their thanks and gratitude with lots of awkwardness, and eventually reached Jose and Maria.

They were surrounded by people, and as I made my way through the mass, I saw that Maria was sitting down and holding Josefina's hand. The old woman was crying but Maria was dry eyed.

"I cannot ever make this up to you," Josefina sobbed.

"You don't need to. We leave in the morning. You can continue your lives and forget this fall out ever happened," Maria said.

Josefina's tears came faster. "Please don't leave. You and Jose belong here with Daniel's memory. I couldn't stand it if you left because of me."

"It wasn't just you," Maria said.

Dozens of people around her muttered apologies and hung their heads in shame.

Maria batted them away with her free hand. "Let it be put behind us. We have known too much suffering in recent times."

"Emily," Jose rose to his feet and pulled me into an embrace. I sank into him and allowed myself to get lost in his smell: coffee and chilli and cinnamon.

"Hey," I murmured.

"You know we have no CCTV, right?" He asked.

I felt my cheeks flush. "Well, I try not to let the truth get in the way of a good interrogation. I wanted him to admit it and give everyone a little closure."

"You did amazing. You were so brave."

"Thank you," I said with a smile.

"You know, I always suspected that my dad's death was an accident. Even though I knew how good a fisherman he was. Nothing else really made sense," Jose said.

"It's a real shame," I said. The words seemed silly as I said them, like the biggest understatement in the world, but Jose seemed to accept them for what they were. An attempt to comfort him, even it was a little clumsy.

"It's better than being killed. As silly as it sounds, just knowing that will give us some comfort."

"I'm glad. You still think you'll leave tomorrow?"

He grinned. "I doubt it. Look at her. She's surrounded by friends. That's all she ever wanted, for this community to accept her again."

"But they've treated her so badly. How will she move on from that?" I asked.

"One day at a time," Jose said.

I followed his gaze and watched as friend after friend approached Maria with coy apologies and nervous hugs. I saw how she greeted each one with a reserved kindness. She hadn't forgotten the way she had been treated, but it was possible to see how the bridges of connection could be rebuilt.

Jose squeezed my hand and returned to her, and I moved away from the crowd and sat alone. Cornelius noticed and wandered over.

"How are you doing, lassie?" He asked.

"I'm doing okay," I said with a smile.

"You look like you have the weight of the world on your shoulders," Cornelius said.

"No, no. I was thinking about mum," I said.

"Ah."

"I think I know what you need to tell me," I said. My voice broke with the words.

"Ah. You really are quite the detective."

"I've just been thinking about the timings. My mum came here when she was 18, and had a holiday romance that I've never heard about. And you told me to remember being proud of her, which makes me think she made a mistake. Or something happened that she wasn't proud of, maybe?"

"Lassie, be careful," Cornelius warned, but it was too late.

"My dad isn't really my dad, is he?" I blurted out.

"He loves you as his daughter. He's your dad in every way that matters," Cornelius said with a squeeze of my hand.

"What happened?" I asked.

Cornelius looked out and I could tell he was replaying memories. "Isadora came home from Mexico walking on air, she was so happy. She had this deep tan and a newfound confidence, and she was completely in love. Things were different back then, no mobile phones and even landline calls were so expensive. It was harder for a holiday romance to continue."

I listened to his words and realised that it made sense. My dad - the dad I'd been raised by - had seemed to pull away from me after my mum's death, because I looked so much like her. I'd never resembled him at all.

"She found out she was expecting you only a few weeks after she got home. She had terrible morning sickness. She always wanted you, lassie. I don't ever want you to doubt that. She loved the bones of you."

"I know," I said. I'd never doubted my mother's love, never in my life.

"It was a different time. A girl who got caught like that was expected to marry the dad, which was never ideal and it just wasn't an option for Isadora. She wrote to your dad but never heard back from him."

"She must have been terrified," I said.

"She was. It was a stigma that could affect a woman's whole life. What your dad did was truly a gift of kindness. Your real dad, not your biological dad."

"He knew?"

Cornelius smiled at the memory. "He'd been sniffing around Isadora for a couple of years with a real case of puppy love. He was besotted with her, lassie. They were best friends growing up and they still were then, but it was clear he was hoping it would develop into more. When she announced the pregnancy, he proposed."

"Just like that?" I exclaimed.

"Oh, he'd have thrown himself under a bus for her!" Cornelius laughed.

"Wow," I said.

"He said he knew she didn't feel the same, but maybe

she would in time. And if she didn't, they'd be married in name only and would raise you as being theirs."

"Even though he knew I wasn't his?" I asked with wide eyes.

Cornelius nodded. "And he was good to his word, lassie. I spent a lot of time with the three of you in those early years. Your dad doted on you. He was a modern man, too! He did some night feeds, he changed nappies, he did it all. He was like a man who couldn't quite believe his luck."

"And what about my mum?"

"At some point, he got his dream come true. Things changed between them. The way she looked at him, it changed. He wasn't just her friend anymore, she fell in love with him. It was beautiful to see."

"She did love him," I agreed. I remembered the two of them dancing in the kitchen as she prepared dinner, or the way they'd hold hands as they sat on a bench at the play-ground watching me go down the slide for the hundredth time.

"And they made a fine couple. To be honest, they've always been my favourite love story, lassie. None of this modern day love at first sight nonsense. Your dad proposing, making a lifelong commitment to Isadora and to you, if that's not the most romantic thing I've ever heard, I don't know what is. You're lucky to have him as a father."

"I know," I said with a smile. I hadn't always been as close to him as I'd wanted to be, at least not since mum's death. Now I wondered whether that was because of this secret. "Why did you and mum fall out?"

"Ah, it was nothing really. Well, to Isadora it must have been. I was of the belief that you had a right to know. Not because I thought you needed this biological dad in your life, but just because I thought it should be your decision. Your mum disagreed. In fact, just the suggestion of it terrified her. She cut me off right away. I think she was scared I'd tell you one day."

"Like you are now?" I asked with a smile.

He let out a chuckle. "Good point. I'm only telling you now with your dad's permission."

"Really? He doesn't mind?"

"He never did, lassie. But he was wise enough to know he wouldn't be the one judged for it if it got out. He's nervous, though. Nervous that you'll want nothing more to do with him. Emily, I know it's a lot to take in."

"I could never cut him off. He's my dad and he always will be. But I have a dad out here. Wow. I can't... I... do you know anything about him?"

Cornelius reached into his backpack and pulled out a slim envelope. I opened it to see a photograph of my mum, ridiculously young and tanned and beautiful, her arms wrapped around a man of a similar age who looked a little like Jose.

"I know, they're similar, right?" Cornelius read my mind.

"We have similar taste," I said with a smile.

"Who wouldn't? Your biological dad was a good looking youngster, and so is Jose."

"This is my dad? It doesn't seem real."

"It will take some time. You were named after him, you know."

"I am?"

"His name's Emilio. Your mum and dad thought it would be a nice acknowledgement, a way of letting you carry part of him with you."

I began to cry as the enormity of the news hit me. I wasn't angry at my mum, I was still proud of her. She had her reasons for not telling me. And I wasn't angry at my dad.

He'd actually acted with more bravery and heroics than I'd ever have expected from him.

"I'll never get to meet him," I said as I looked at the photograph in front of me. While I might not ever consider that man to be my father, I was curious. Did I have any of his mannerisms? Would I meet him and feel a connection? But there was no way I would be able to track him down from that single photograph and a first name.

Cornelius grinned at me. "Turn over the photo, lassie."

I did as he said and there, in a faint scrawl that I recognised instantly as belonging to my mother, was a few lines of writing.

It was my father's address.

~

THE END

~

To continue reading Emily and Uncle C's adventures, get your copy of Here Today, Gone Tomato!

UNCLE C'S WORLD WIDE WEB LOG

E (or not E) has the address.

What will her next move be, wise old internet?

Shall we move on to the resort I'd chosen for us?

Or will we venture into the unknown?

Yes, this does all sound very cryptic. But if I can't reveal Emily's name to you, I certainly can't share more than this.

I see a glint in her eyes. I suspect she will be allowing this old dog a few more adventures yet.

There's one thing I know for certain. We won't be returning to the hotel. It was a stroke of pure luck bumping into Luis! I managed to persuade him to pack up our belongings and meet us back on the mainland.

Well, there was no way this old adventurer could sit through a boring investment meeting, was there?! ;-)

Until next time,

Uncle C

ABOUT THE AUTHOR

Mona Marple is author of the Waterfell Tweed, Mystic Springs and Christmas Corpse cozy mystery series', a co-author of the Witch in Time series, and author of the Moonstone Hollow paranormal women's fiction series.

She lives in Nottinghamshire, England with her daughter, husband and pampered Labradoodle.

When she isn't writing words, Mona is probably reading them. She also enjoys walking, being by the sea, and spending quality time with her loved ones.

facebook.com/MonaMarpleAuthor
instagram.com/monamarple